A TRAIL TO WOUNDED KNEE

Also by Tim Champlin
in Large Print:

Shadow Catcher
Lincoln's Ransom
Great Timber Race
The Tombstone Conspiracy
Treasure of the Templars
Wayfaring Strangers
Flying Eagle
The Survivor
Swift Thunder
The Last Campaign
Deadly Season
Colt Lightning
King of the Highbinders
Summer of the Sioux

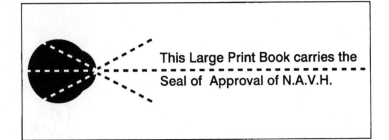

A TRAIL TO WOUNDED KNEE

A Western Story

Tim Champlin

Thorndike Press • Waterville, Maine

Published in 2002 by arrangement with
Golden West Literary Agency.

Thorndike Press Large Print Western Series.

The tree indicium is a trademark of Thorndike Press.

The text of this Large Print edition is unabridged.
Other aspects of the book may vary from the original edition.

Cover design by Thorndike Press Staff.

Set in 16 pt. Plantin by Rick Gundberg.

Printed in the United States on permanent paper.

Library of Congress Cataloging-in-Publication Data

Champlin, Tim, 1937–
  A trail to Wounded Knee : a Western story / Tim
Champlin.
    p. cm.
  ISBN 0-7862-2402-9 (lg. print : hc : alk. paper)
  1. Pine Ridge Indian Reservation (S.D.) — Fiction.
  2. Wounded Knee Massacre, S.D., 1890 — Fiction.
  3. Dakota Indians — Fiction. 4. South Dakota — Fiction.
  5. Ghost dance — Fiction. 6. Large type books. I. Title.
  PS3553.H265 T73 2002
  813′.54—dc21   2001041544

For my grandson
Sawyer E. Champlin

Prologue

With the last surrender of Geronimo in 1886, the subjugation of the war-like American Indian tribes was nearly complete. Only a few years before, the various Sioux tribes of the northern plains had been herded onto reservations, their old nomadic way of life eliminated within the space of a lifetime by vastly superior numbers and firepower.

More than any one thing, the deliberate extermination of the buffalo ended the Sioux (Lakota) way of life. The plains Indians were dependent on this animal for food, clothing, shelter, and implements. It also figured into their religious ceremonies. By 1888, only about one thousand buffalo remained of the estimated thirteen million that had roamed the plains less than thirty years before. Without the buffalo, the whole Indian culture had to change. By the late 1880s, the Sioux had been forced to give up the Black Hills and large tracts of their original reservations for white settlement.

Official U.S. government policy of dealing with the Sioux, and others once the natives' old way of life had been crushed, involved an attempt to make them over into "civilized" wards. This the government expected to accomplish by turning them into settled, subsistence farmers, by taking their children into boarding schools or reservation day schools, cutting their hair, dressing them in white man's clothing, teaching them English and the values of American society. The adults were given plows and seeds and instructions for planting and harvesting. Never mind that the western Dakotas were more suited to grazing than to growing crops. Long-standing traditions concerning marriage were forbidden. Traditional ways of showing grief were banned. Christian missionaries of various denominations proselytized with considerable success on the Lakota reservations to displace the old gods.

Indians who co-operated with this approach to a new life style were labeled "Progressives," while those who resisted by various means were termed "Nonprogressives." By 1890, many of the young adult Indians knew nothing but dominant white culture and reservation life. And many of the older ones realized there was nothing left for them but to follow the white man's road or starve to death.

A civilian agent was put in charge of each

reservation by the U.S. Department of the Interior. The main requirement for attaining one of these appointed positions was the correct political affiliation. No experience with Indians was required. The few good agents, such as John Clum of the Apache San Carlos reservation in Arizona and James McLaughlin of the Standing Rock Lakota reservation in North Dakota, were vastly outnumbered by the incompetent and downright dishonest agents in other places. As a result, the beef issue was often short, either because of thievery or because Congress failed to appropriate sufficient money to buy enough food to fulfill treaty obligations.

The Sioux by 1890 were thoroughly beaten and demoralized. Distrust of promises made by the Americans, fear of having their meager food supply cut off if they caused any kind of trouble, unable or unwilling to take up farming and the habits of white culture, the loss of a roaming, hunting, warring way of life — all of these combined with poverty and disease to make the Sioux ripe for some kind of savior, anything to provide them with hope for the future.

In 1889, at about the time despair and actual starvation were afflicting many of the Sioux, there arose a Paiute Indian in western Nevada named Wovoka who claimed to have been granted visions by God. Known as Jack Wilson to the whites in whose culture he had been reared, there was nothing of the radical visionary about him. Yet he came to believe, and then to teach, that the Christian Messiah had appeared to him, promising He would return and restore the Indian people to their former glory and would eliminate the white people. In order to bring this about, Wovoka said the Messiah instructed him to have all Indian people dance a special dance, to pray, and to harm no one. The subjugated Indian tribes took to this new religion like drowning people to a lifeboat, and the new dance religion spread rapidly. The Sioux on the Lakota reservations heard about it within several weeks. Out of curiosity, the older leaders sent a delegation to far-off Nevada to investigate and bring back a report. The eleven-man delegation consisted of Good Thunder, Yellow Breast, Flat Iron, Broken Arm, Cloud Horse, Yellow Knife, Elk Horn, and Kicks Back from the Pine Ridge reservation, along with Mash-The-Kettle and Short Bull of the Rosebud reservation, and Kicking Bear from the Cheyenne River reservation. When the delegation returned, they brought an accurate report — with one exception. To the new religion they added the teaching that the special ghost dance shirts the people were to wear would render the dancers bulletproof. The Sioux were the only Indians who believed or taught this.

The spring of 1890 brought good rains, and the crops got off to a promising start. Other aspects of Lakota reservation life were not rosy, but at least those who'd planted might have sufficient food for the year. By midsummer, however, the rains ceased, and the high plains were being baked by a merciless sun. Hot winds shriveled the crops, and the Indians began killing their breeding stock for food and eating their seed grain. In desperation, many of them turned to the ghost dance in hopes the Messiah would return and give them a better life.

Chapter One

April, 1876
Fifteen miles northwest of
Fort Hartsuff, Nebraska

"What took you so long?" The lean, leathery rancher named Watson leaned his rifle against the outside wall of the cottonwood log ranch house and wiped his face with a shirt sleeve.

Lt. Thaddeus Coyle choked back a sharp retort when he saw the man was nearly in tears. "We got here as quick as we could," he replied.

The rancher jerked his head toward the door. "My brother dead, two kids wounded. Damn' Sioux caught Charley near the barn. They just rode in without no warning and started shooting and burning."

Through the open plank door, Coyle could hear a woman's muffled sobbing. He clenched his teeth in silent frustration. It had been the same years before when he'd served against the Apaches in Arizona Territory — the barbaric raiders struck like lightning, then faded back into the landscape, frustrating all Army attempts to catch and punish them.

Just after reveille this morning a messenger had slid his lathered horse to a stop in front of the adjutant's office at the fort, yelling something about an Indian attack on the settlers. Major Adrian Spandell had ordered Coyle to mount two dozen of the post's infantrymen and ride to the relief of the whites. Seasoned cavalry would have been in the saddle and on their way within a quarter hour. It took the infantry nearly three times that long before they rode out of the parade ground that was enclosed by the fort's cement buildings. Coyle had chafed under the delay, knowing the major's eyes were watching their every bumbling move from the front porch of his office. Small as the detail was, it represented more than a quarter of Fort Hartsuff's one under-strength unit — Company A of the 23rd infantry. Despite constant training, most of these men knew little horsemanship. Horses were used only to transport them to the scene of action more quickly than marching. In this wide-open country of vast distances, mounted infantry was usually a necessity.

The hostiles had been quiet for several months through the winter, and many soldiers at this outpost on the eastern edge of the

Nebraska sandhills were eager for anything that would break their routine of drill and stable duty. However, more than a few of the two dozen men were apprehensive at the thought of their first hostile action. Coyle, however, had doubted they would see any fighting that day.

"Well, aren't you gonna take out after 'em?" the lean man demanded. "You gonna just let 'em get away with killin' my brother? We held 'em off till you come."

Coyle had himself well in hand now and made no response to the man's irritated tone. He looked around at the smoldering ruins of the barn, the woodshed, and the outhouse. "Sergeant Daugherty, get the men mounted. We should be able to pick up their trail."

He swung up into the saddle as the non-com relayed the command. It had been a hard ride of fifteen miles from the fort, and some of the soldiers groaned and muttered under their breaths as they struggled to remount. Rancher Watson indicated the direction the Sioux had taken, and Coyle led out with 1st Sgt. Daugherty riding at his stirrup. Once they were away from the ranch buildings, the trail in the sand of the grassy hills was easy enough to pick up. From the tracks, Daugherty estimated their quarry numbered about thirty.

The raiding party, in a hurry or just disdainful of pursuit, had made no attempt to hide their trail in the loose soil. Two miles out, Coyle and his detail came across the fresh carcasses of two slaughtered Herefords. Coyle halted the column and climbed down to have a look.

"They cut off a few hunks of meat to eat on the way. About as wasteful as whites killing the buffalo."

"Anything to drive off the whites and their animals," Daugherty commented as Coyle swung up onto the saddle. "They're mad as hell."

"Watson said they were painted up for war." Coyle added, pulling on his gauntlets: "Send one of the men back to tell the ranchers they can salvage this beef."

The trail led across the sandhills in a northwesterly direction. An hour later, Coyle halted the column so the horses could drink from a reed-bordered lake cupped in a hollow of the hills. To prevent any surprises, he posted two scouts on the crest of the hill in front and one behind. Ten minutes later, they were once again on the trail. He didn't push the pace, knowing their mounts were not the best he'd ever seen, and it was a long walk back to the post. From the slurred tracks, he could tell the Sioux were moving at a much faster pace. Treeless, open country now surrounded them, the grassy sandhills like huge ocean waves arrested in their heaving motion. He paused now and then to uncase his field glasses and scan the terrain ahead for sign of their quarry. The dunes stretched away to the horizon with no moving thing visible, but he guessed the Indians were probably following the easier lowlands between the hills. All that kept this unique area from appearing as a vast desert was the presence of the stabilizing grass and the presence of a high water table. The many small ponds and lakes drew thousands of migrating waterfowl.

"Sergeant Daugherty, send out three men to ride point and scout."

"Yes, sir." Daugherty turned in his saddle. "Carson! Lewis! Farnham! Ride ahead about four hundred yards. Stay in sight of the column and keep your eyes peeled for that war party. Have your weapons handy, but don't fire. Give an arm signal or ride back here on the double, if you see anything."

"Right, Sergeant."

The three men pulled their mounts out of line.

"Carson!" Lt. Coyle snapped. "Quit sawing that horse's mouth with the reins! He's already skittish. Get back in the column." He turned to his right. "Sergeant, send another man in his place."

As Coyle turned back, Carson was galloping away with the first two soldiers. "Carson!" Coyle shouted, but the corporal gave no indication he'd heard. "Damnation!" Coyle exploded under his breath. He'd see to it that Carson did extra duty for disobeying a direct order.

Meanwhile, Daugherty ordered out a fourth man who was spurring after the first three.

Even though the Indians' tracks curved among the hills, Coyle hoped to cut off some distance by going in a direct line, up and down the hills. He knew he couldn't keep this up for long because of the fatigue of the horses. If he didn't spot the fleeing Indians soon, he'd have to turn back to the fort.

Less than an hour later they caught up with the war party. The first indication of trouble was a burst of gunfire from beyond the next hill. Coyle saw Cpl. Carson throw up his hands as his horse plunged ahead with him. The soldier's feet flew out of the stirrups, and the panicked mount went charging ahead over the crest of the hill and out of sight. The three other scouts spurred their horses back toward the column.

"At a gallop, ho!" Lt. Coyle shouted, spurring his horse to a dead run down the sloping hillside and across the shallow swale, the column at his back. Just as they topped the next rise, he saw Carson's horse, still out of control, galloping back toward them, carrying the corporal through the scattering Sioux warriors. The Indians were grabbing for their plunging ponies and trying to fire at him with their Winchesters.

Carson, revolver in hand, was firing left and right as his wounded mount, dragging the reins, labored up the slope toward the column.

"Dismount and fire!" Coyle yelled. "Prone position!"

"Every fourth man . . . get hold of those horses!" Sgt. Daugherty shouted. "Don't let 'em get away!"

The infantrymen threw themselves onto their bellies, leveling their single-shot Springfield rifles at the Sioux below who appeared surprised by the sudden appearance of the blue coats.

Coyle, on one knee just below the lip of the hill, fired his long-barreled Colt into the surging mass of horses and warriors. In the roar of rifle fire, smoke, shouting, and the squealing of horses, everything in Coyle's perception seemed to slow down. Sound faded, and the figures around him appeared to be moving very slowly. He could see everything clearly. Afoot, most of these infantrymen had one big

advantage over any foe, mounted or other-
wise — they were dead shots with their Long
Toms.

As Carson's spooked horse labored up the
sandy slope, blood-streaked flanks heaving, it
suddenly collapsed onto its side, falling
heavily on its rider before he could kick free.

Sgt. Daugherty saw what was happening
and dashed to the pinned soldier. Coyle saw
the big sergeant grab Carson under both arms
and heave backward, digging in his heels.
Two Sioux, who were no more than forty
yards away, raised their rifles and aimed at
Daugherty. Coyle fired his pistol at one and
saw the warrior drop his rifle and grab his
thigh. At the same instant, smoke spurted
from the Winchester of the other, and Coyle
saw the sergeant flop onto his back, and lie
still.

Coyle swore and cocked his pistol, taking
careful aim. The hammer fell on a spent shell.
But the fire of the infantry was beginning to
tell as four Indians dropped, and the rest,
some wounded, vaulted onto their ponies'
backs. In less than a minute they were galloping up the far slope, firing wildly back over
their shoulders with the short carbines.

Suddenly it was over. The last feathered
head disappeared below the waving grass of
the next hill, followed by three more booming

19

shots from the Springfields. In the abrupt silence, wind shredded and dissipated clouds of acrid gunsmoke.

The soldiers, who'd never been under fire, cheered as if they'd just defeated the whole Sioux nation, pounded each other on the back, and stood up, shaking their rifles overhead.

"Shut up!" Coyle roared. "See to your weapons and keep your heads down!"

Cursing under his breath, Coyle plunged down the slope on foot, sliding to a stop where Carson still lay on his side, struggling to free his left leg from under the dead horse. One look at Sgt. Daugherty told Coyle he was beyond help.

"Get me out from under this damned horse, Lieutenant!" Carson whined. "I think my leg's busted."

Coyle looked at the man as if he weren't even there, rose to his feet, holstering his Colt, and walked back up the hill. "Jackson! Stevens! Garfield! Get him out from under that horse!" he ordered, jerking his thumb over his shoulder. He stopped at the crest of the hill and caught sight of the fleeing war party in the distance. They were leaving four of their number sprawled in the sand at the bottom of the hill, along with two dead horses. If the vultures and coyotes didn't get the bodies first, the Sioux would return for their dead comrades. Coyle was so angry, he hardly noticed the bodies. "That fool, Carson, cost me the best sergeant I ever had," he muttered under his breath. Then aloud: "Bring Sergeant Daugherty's body up here. Wrap him in a blanket and tie him across his saddle."

He looked back down into the hollow where the bodies of the Sioux and their ponies lay in a bare patch of sand known as a blowout. Where the grass was thin and there was little to anchor the loose soil, swirling winds had scoured out large depressions of bare sand. "The battle of the blowout," Coyle muttered, thinking of what he would have to write of this incident in his report. Maybe by tomorrow his anger at Cpl. Carson would have cooled.

Lt. Coyle walked into his Spartan office at Fort Hartsuff's administration building the next morning, feeling as if he'd been pounded by a horse's hoofs. He took a long sip of the coffee from the thick mug he carried and sat down at his desk, wondering about his physical conditioning. The long ride and the fight should not have made him this sore and stiff.

The spring sun slanted through the window and threw a splash of brilliance across the top of the old wooden desk. The atmosphere was much brighter than his mood. The clash with the Sioux had been the worst in the three years since this fort had been established. The soldiers were here to furnish protection for the white settlers and the friendly Indians in the area. He'd done his job to the best of his ability, yet he felt as if he'd somehow failed and didn't relish writing the report of yesterday's action. Even though the hostiles had been stung by the loss of four dead and several wounded, he had the nagging feeling that, if he'd done his job better, he would not have lost Sgt. Daugherty.

His gaze fell on a sheet of paper on his desk. Distractedly he picked it up and glanced at the printed document. The words made his stomach contract. It was a recommendation for the Congressional Medal of Honor for Cpl. Thomas Carson! It was worded as if Coyle had written it, prepared for his signature. He reread the document vaguely.

. . . demonstrated undaunted courage in the face of overwhelming hostile Sioux Indians. . . . attacked the war party single-handed to give his column of mounted infantry time to prepare for battle . . . horse was shot from under him, falling on Corporal Carson, breaking his

22

leg. . . . We most sincerely recommend that the exemplary courage of this soldier in saving his comrades from surprise attack be recognized by considering him for the Congressional Medal of Honor.

> Signed:
> Thaddeus Coyle,
> First Lieutenant,
> Company A, 23rd infantry
> Concurred in:
> Adrian G. Spandell,
> Major, Commanding,
> Fort Hartsuff, Nebraska

A space had been left for Coyle's signature above the printed name and title. He was incredulous. Never could he sign such a document. It was a falsehood from beginning to end. If anything, just the opposite was true. Carson, by losing control of his mount, had actually been responsible for the death of Sgt. Daugherty. Coyle felt sick. He knew what this meant. If the incident had been handled properly, Major Spandell would have called him in and discussed the whole affair before deciding to recommend anyone for such an honor. The fact that this document had been written, printed, and laid on his desk for him to find, read, and sign was just another way

Spandell was telling him he lacked leadership capability, that his battlefield commission, granted toward the end of the War Between the States, had been a mistake — a fluke.

Cpl. Carson was one of those soldiers who was constantly malingering, always in trouble for various infractions, from being drunk on duty to smuggling a prostitute into the barracks. His guardhouse time had probably equaled his good time. He had been busted to private twice. It was over Coyle's objections that the major had restored him to the rank of corporal.

Coyle stared with unseeing eyes at the document before him. This was undoubtedly the work of his superior officer who had composed the document and ordered it printed up overnight. But what had Major Spandell to gain by this? Maybe if the War Department saw him as a leader of such heroic men, they would recommend him for the next colonel's vacancy and promote him away from this obscure frontier post to some more prestigious command.

The only other possibility was one Coyle hardly dared consider — Spandell was sexually attracted to Carson. When in his cups at various social functions, the plump major, by surreptitious word and gesture, had let slip what his inclinations were toward this handsome younger man. Perhaps that was why, in spite of Carson's repeated offenses, including such things as disobeying direct orders, sleeping while on guard duty, and fighting, the man had not been dishonorably discharged for the good of the service. He had a protector in high places.

"Mister Coyle, please come to my office."

Coyle cringed at the sound of the familiar voice as his commander passed the open door. He took a deep breath and got up without hesitation. *Might as well get this over with,* he thought. He knew what was coming and steeled himself for the confrontation.

"Close the door."

Coyle obeyed, and stood at parade rest before the big desk. Even though there was a straight wooden chair in the office, the major did not invite him to sit down.

"You saw the document on your desk?"

"Yes, sir."

"Sign it right away. I want to send it off by special courier this morning."

"I haven't given you my report of the fight yet."

"You can attend to that later," the major said with a dismissive wave of one pudgy hand. He sat back in the big desk chair and crossed his legs. The rotund body stretched the dark blue fabric of the uniform. Sparse blond hair was combed carefully across the pink skull. Freshly shaven cheeks rounded into a smooth roll of double chin above the high-collared tunic. A graying blond mustache hid all of his mouth but a petulant lower lip. "Do you have any questions?"

"I can't sign that recommendation, sir." He held his breath for the explosion.

Like a fat cat waiting for a captured mouse to run, the major sprang on him. "You *will* sign it, Lieutenant Coyle. That's an order."

Coyle tried again, softening his tone, speaking to a fellow officer. "Sir, you and I both know that's not what happened." *Better to leave Carson's record out of this and stick to the facts,* he thought. "Due to the rolling nature of the terrain, I ordered Sergeant Daugherty to send three outriders ahead of us. In case we were closing with the war party, I wanted the scouts to spot them first before the column came up."

"Why? To give them a chance to run?" The tone was derisive.

Coyle ignored the remark and hurried on. "No, sir. As you know, infantry can't fight on horseback with their long Springfields. But those rifles are accurate up to a thousand yards, so I knew the advantage would be with us, if we could deal with the hostiles from long range."

The pouches of fat under the cold gray eyes were slightly puffier than usual, Coyle thought. Probably from lack of sleep if the major had been up late in the print shop.

"Anyway, I noticed that Carson's mount was acting up and that he was mishandling the animal, so I ordered him back in line and told the sergeant to send someone else. As soon as I turned my back, Carson disobeyed my direct order and rode off, anyway. I yelled, but he didn't come back."

"Maybe he didn't hear the order."

"Not a chance, sir."

"If you consider Tom Carson a poor horseman, why did you mount him on such a fractious animal?"

Coyle had no ready answer.

"Continue," the major said, when Coyle hesitated.

"Anyway, the scouts spotted the hostiles in a swale between two hills where they'd stopped to water their horses in a pond. I assume the Indians weren't expecting any pursuit and weren't watching their back trail. Three of the four scouts waved and immediately turned and rode back toward the column. Carson told me later his horse spooked at the first shot and went charging down the hill right into the Sioux. Carson panicked and lost the reins and the stirrups, but had the

27

presence of mind to fire his one rifle shot, then pull his revolver. By some miracle of surprise and luck, he rode right through them and wasn't hit. But then the horse, apparently realizing that none of his stable mates was nearby, turned and galloped back through the Sioux, who by this time were trying to get hold of their stampeded horses and still shoot at this attacking soldier." Coyle had abandoned his stiff posture and was moving and gesturing as he recalled the scene.

"The horse was acting on its own?" Spandell asked, with some sarcasm.

"That's what Carson told me. The column was at the gallop by this time. Just as we reached the crest of the hill, Carson's horse came struggling up through the sand. The animal had been struck several times and fell about forty yards short of the column, pinning Carson underneath. Sergeant Daugherty ran to help but was shot dead." Coyle paused. "If anyone deserves a medal, it's Daugherty. He might never know, but his wife and kids would."

"You say Carson was firing his pistol as he rode?"

"Yes, sir. He said he didn't even remember doing it, though. Instinct for self-preservation, I expect."

"You don't assume anything, mister. We

will stick to the facts, here." The moist lower lip stuck out beneath the mustache as the major uncrossed his legs and leaned forward in his chair. "From everything you've described, Carson's actions were those of a hero."

"Carson would not have been there if he had not disobeyed my direct order. His actions were completely involuntary. He told me so himself. His horse should be given the medal, if one is due at all."

"Are you making a joke of this?" The voice was icy.

"No, sir."

"As you well know from your own experience, the actions that make heroes are not always planned in advance, nor reasoned out while they are being performed."

The major's allusions to Coyle's battlefield promotion for gallantry and selfless acts at the Battle of Franklin rankled him, but he didn't let on. They had lost an excellent career sergeant and a good man, yet this fat, self-serving man had not even mentioned Daugherty's death. Coyle's dislike intensified. He and the major had been at odds for months, but Coyle suspected his written request for transfer had never been forwarded to higher authority. He thought the major would be glad to be rid of him, except that the post ran well because of

Coyle's popularity with the men.

In a change of tack, the major got up, came around the desk, and put a hand on Coyle's shoulder. "Thaddeus, this country needs heroes. You and I would be derelict in our duty as soldiers if we didn't provide them at every legitimate opportunity."

Coyle grimaced at the transparent familiarity.

"Why don't you just go ahead and sign it?" Major Spandell said. "You can also recommend any other men in your detail you feel are deserving."

"I can't sign that, sir. You are his commanding officer. You can sign it if you wish."

"You know it has to be signed by the officer who witnessed the action," Spandell said. "You are his immediate superior, and you were there. The facts as written are essentially correct." The major paused and softened his voice once more. "You and I will be advancing our careers and doing Carson and the Army a favor all at once. Just sign the recommendation and let's get on with it."

"I didn't write that recommendation, sir, and I don't believe it's warranted."

"Sign the damn' paper, man, or face the consequences!" It was apparent the major was quickly losing patience, his round cheeks flushing pink. "I'll expect that signed docu-

30

ment on my desk by noon mess or. . . ."

"Or what?"

"By God, how does the word insubordination sound to you? You are no more officer material than my horse!" he spat derisively. He pulled a handkerchief from his pocket and wiped at the spittle that was escaping his lower lip.

A red veil of fury descended across Coyle's eyes. He knew the danger signal well, but could no more heed the warning than he could have made himself invisible. "Sign the damned thing yourself, you fat son-of-a-bitch! I won't be a party to your lies!" Coyle turned on his heel, yanked the door open, and stalked out.

Instead of returning to his office, Coyle plunged blindly outside into the morning sunshine and fresh air. His feet took him across the parade ground and into the post infirmary. He was hardly aware of the three wounded privates who lay on cots and of another man who sat on a chair, holding a swollen jaw. He slumped down on a chair in a corner and leaned weakly against the wall, trembling with suppressed rage. Whatever the consequences, he had thrown down the gauntlet.

Just then his old friend, Dr. Stuart Mecklenburg, walked in the door. "Thad, what ails you this morning?" he asked brightly. "You got diarrhea, too?" He grinned. "Let me see to these patients, and we'll go have coffee." Then he looked closer at Coyle's face. "Come in here a minute." He nodded toward an adjoining room.

Coyle followed his friend and confidant, the forty-year old post surgeon, into the next room. The doctor closed the door. "What's the matter?" he asked in a low, serious tone.

In a choked voice, Coyle briefly related the situation.

Mecklenburg leaned against a cabinet lined with medicine bottles and folded his arms across his chest. He didn't speak for a long minute, while Coyle tried to get his emotions under control. "I know Corporal Carson well. He reports for sick call every day or two with some new ailment he's concocted. But is he really worth losing your career over? I set his leg last night. It was a clean break just below the knee . . . which was also wrenched badly. Probably severely torn ligaments. It's possible he'll have a limp after the leg fracture heals in a few months. Not likely he'll be allowed to reënlist in the infantry. He'll be a civilian soon, and the whole matter will be forgotten." When Coyle didn't reply, he went on. "What difference does it make, anyway? Washington might not even accept the recommendation for the medal. Who knows? But you know how the old man is. He could court-martial you over this. He's a bear for military discipline. Why don't you just sign the thing and forget it?"

"The other men in this company respect me, Stuart. They saw what happened. I even heard them discussing it and laughing about it on the ride back. What would they think of me, if I put my name to such a thing?"

Dr. Mecklenburg nodded. "But you have your own career to think about. You're due for a captaincy when a slot opens up. Rank has been mighty hard to make since the big cutback after the war." He shrugged. "It's nothing earth-shaking. Why don't you just obey orders and sign it? Save yourself a lot of trouble over nothing. Who's to know the difference?"

"I will," Coyle replied. "I have to live inside this skin. I don't mean to sound self-righteous, but lying and dishonesty are not two of my failings, especially when it comes to my official duty."

"Well, all I can say is Diogenes can put down his lantern when he meets up with you." He opened the glass-fronted door of the medicine cabinet and took out a brown bottle of camphor and a wad of cotton. "I don't mean to sound flippant. I really admire your honesty. But courage goes along with conviction. Everything in life has a price. I just hope this doesn't cost you more than you can afford."

Chapter Two

June 13, 1876
Southwestern Dakota Territory

It had been five days since the court-martial verdict in Omaha — five days since Coyle's life had been shattered. He'd been stripped of all rank and dishonorably discharged from the United States Army, his career ended after sixteen years of continuous active service as enlisted man and officer. Impeccably dressed in his blue uniform that proudly displayed his first lieutenant's shoulder straps, he'd sat through two days of testimony leading up to the decision by the panel of officers. Even when the verdict was handed down, to the obvious delight of Major Spandell, he'd kept up an impassive front, never displaying any outward emotion.

It was the second blow, two hours later, that had nearly killed him. His wife, Emma, who attended the trial with their two children, Bradley and Jill, announced she was leaving him. He and Emma were alone in a room that had been assigned to him and his attorney to prepare his case. It was just down the hall from where the court sat. There was a charged silence between Coyle and his wife as he changed into civilian clothing brought from Fort Hartsuff. The two children, ages four and six, were under the watchful eye of an enlisted man outside in the hallway.

He had folded his uniform for the last time and laid it on the table, thinking that, at least, he'd been spared the ignominy of being drummed out of the service. That was a formal ceremony designed to impress, but one that was rarely performed any more, except for a man who'd committed some heinous offense. In those cases, the verdict was read aloud and the unfortunate soldier had the insignia of his rank and his brass buttons ripped off. Then, as the drummers beat a long roll, the assembled troops did an about-face and turned their backs on the convicted man as he walked off the post in public disgrace.

"What are you going to do now?" Emma had asked in a tired voice, not looking at him.

"Let's go home. It'll be nice spending a little time with my family."

"They took away all your pay, even what you were due for accumulated leave. What are we going to live on?" Her voice had sounded cold, detached.

36

"I . . . I'll get a job."

"Doing what?"

No word of support, no encouragement. He had pushed ahead as if he hadn't detected the chill. "I'm not sure just yet. Something will turn up." It was an unsettling thought to be suddenly thrown onto the labor market at the age of thirty-four with no saleable skills. He'd have to find common labor, he supposed, until he could retrain himself for something better.

"What kind of job can you get after you've been put out of the Army?"

He had dropped his pretense. "Emma, what's wrong? Didn't you want me to stand up for my beliefs? What kind of man do you think I am?"

"One who should be able to provide for his family." She had still averted her eyes from him.

"I thought I'd been doing that since we married." She was concerned strictly with practicalities, he had thought. No mention of love, or pride, or principle.

"Two thousand a year just won't do it. I've had to scrub floors to make ends meet. We've never even had a house of our own. And you're gone all the time to some god-forsaken post in the middle of nowhere."

"You could have come and lived with me at

Fort Hartsuff," he had said. "The quarters there are pretty decent for an officer's family."

"What kind of life is that for the kids? Bradley's of school age, and Jill will be shortly."

"Well, all that's behind us now," he had said, forcing cheerfulness. "We'll be a family again. As soon as I get a job, I'll get you out of that boarding house, and. . . ." His voice had trailed off as he saw her shaking her head.

"Thad, I wanted you to get out of the Army when we married. But, no, you took the easy way . . . instead of showing some ambition and getting a real job where you could make some money and take care of your family. And now this disgrace that'll follow you for the rest of your life! What kind of job can you get with a dishonorable discharge on your record?"

She had accused him of taking the easy way? He thought bitterly of the hostile fire he'd faced, the tongue-lashings received from superiors, the postings to remote forts with primitive facilities where he'd often crawled out of a bunk on winter mornings when it was twenty below, the discipline problems he'd had to deal with.

Apparently she had taken his silence for hesitancy or indecision. "I think we should separate for a while," she had continued, driving a knife into his heart. "I'll take the kids and go back to live with my mother in Denison, Iowa. She can use my help since Dad died, and Brad and Jill will have a nice home and a place to go to school. Mother's always been crazy about the kids."

"What about me?" he had heard himself asking.

"When you get your life together, you know where we'll be. Maybe by then the children will have forgotten about all this mess. I'm not sure they understood it, anyway. And kids at their age are pretty resilient."

"Are you leaving right away?" he had asked, his voice sounding forlorn.

"We don't have much to pack. We'll take the train in the morning. I've already telegraphed mother. She's expecting us."

"I wish you wouldn't do this. We can get along and work this out." He would've begged if necessary. Anything to have kept his life from falling completely to ruin.

"No. Our plans are made for now. Good bye, Thad." No kiss, no touch of her hand, hardly even a look.

She had walked out the door, taking the children before he got a chance to tell them good bye. He had followed them outside. When Jill waved at him from the carriage window as they drove away, he'd almost wished the stab of anguish he felt were actually a fatal heart attack.

Coyle reined up his walking mount, took a deep breath of the fresh prairie air, and savored the silence for a minute before dismounting. He was still reliving the pain of last week's military disgrace and personal separation. His mind had repressed most of the details of the remainder of that fateful day and, also, of the next. It all had a dream-like quality, but he vaguely recalled going through the motions to quit the post as a civilian.

He'd ridden back to Fort Hartsuff on a strong four year-old gelding he'd purchased in Omaha. He stood now beside the well-trained bay and ran a hand over the brand on its hip — IC — Inspected and Condemned, the military mark for a horse that was unfit for service. In this case, the bay could not be trained to ignore the explosive noise of gunfire. "Both of us . . . rejected," he muttered, patting the animal's neck. "We'll make a good pair." He smiled at the irony of it as he led the horse toward a small pond cupped in a swale in the prairie. The pond was several yards across and fringed with tall reeds on one side. He'd been in the saddle since daylight, and now the sun was nearly overhead, but the June temperature was only in the seventies.

He slipped the bit from the horse's mouth so the animal would become accustomed to graze only when not under control of the reins. Then he loosened the girth. He rummaged in the saddlebags for a pair of hobbles and attached them to the bay's front hoofs — less comfortable for the horse, but more secure than a picket pin in loose soil.

He took a few long strides up the slope to take a look around. He wished he'd thought to bring a pair of field glasses as he slitted his eyes beneath his hat brim and scanned the open country, turning slowly in a complete circle. Off to the north, in the middle distance, he spotted two tiny fawn-colored spots he finally identified as grazing antelope. Except for that and a hawk, soaring high overhead, he might have been alone on the earth. He inhaled deeply of the honey-scented breeze. He'd been smelling this same delightful fragrance since yesterday, and pulled a handful of tiny yellow flowers from a nearby plant that grew nearly waist-high. He sniffed the flowers. That was it — yellow honey clover. It was perfuming the air for miles around. Yellow swatches of it were growing wild here and there on the grassland as far as he could see. In his experience, this plant didn't bloom in such profusion every year. There had to be an abundance of spring rain. The past couple of months had been wetter than usual, and that also accounted for the many small watering holes he'd encountered. Two small rivers he'd had to cross were running swift and high with pewter-colored silt. But this day there was no sign of rain. In fact, the mare's tails streaking the deep blue heavens were an almost sure sign of fair weather for the next couple of days.

He was headed west to the gold-rush town of Deadwood, in the Black Hills, another two or three days away. He'd been conservative long enough, he decided. He would become one of those get-rich-quick prospectors. After all, he had nothing left to lose. He was free of all constraint and could try anything that suited his fancy. It was an odd feeling, being completely footloose. Never, since he'd enlisted as a private during the war, had he been free of the weight of duty and obligation. Everything he owned was on his back or in his saddlebags. The saddle his bay carried was a used Army McClellan, lightweight, but comfortably shaped. A well-worn Winchester carbine hung in a scabbard, and he carried his Army issue Colt .45 on his hip. With foresight, he'd bought a rifle that used the same cartridges as his revolver.

He went back to the horse, that was grazing contentedly, and fished around in the saddlebags for the bread that was on the verge of becoming moldy, along with strips of dried beef. He detached his canteen and took his lunch back up onto a level area above the pond where he could keep watch. Freedom, after all, didn't mean he ceased to be cautious. Never had any food tasted so good as this simple meal, washed down with plain water. Several miles to the west he could make out buff-colored buttes and mesas topped with a scattering of pine trees — the broken, eroded eastern edge of the Badlands. He would feel a little safer once he got into them. He loved the prairie, but he could be spotted a long way off by Indians. He might make an inviting target for any war-like bucks who happened to spot him in this remote, open country.

When he finished eating, he stretched out in the grass and picked his teeth with the stem of a weed. There was no sound but the soft soughing of the south wind through the grass that grew a foot tall, but was not thick. He doubted that antelope and other wild creatures appreciated the beauty of their surroundings. Their environment meant only a source of food and shelter to them. Humans were likely the only species who had the power of intellect to reflect on their own surroundings, to be aware of its beauty, apart from its ability to supply basic physical needs.

But the downside was that humans were, also, the only ones who could recall and reflect on emotional hurts, thus causing themselves to suffer anew.

Coyle knew he was a man who did not make friends easily. Even though he was friendly enough, he didn't possess the personality that encouraged others to confide in him, possibly one of the defects that had eroded his marriage. But he had been blessed with an unusually good memory for detail and a remarkably good imagination. Both had been a source of great pleasure and pain in the past. Now he called upon them to recreate a concert he'd attended in Omaha six months earlier — to affect an escape from his present emotional pain. While on Christmas leave, he and Emma had attended a concert where the orchestra had performed an evening of music by Ludwig van Beethoven.

As he lay there, fingers laced behind his head and stared at the clouds, the sibilant sighing of wind in the prairie grass slowly slid into the smooth sound of violins. Then woodwinds blended in, followed by the brass of a large orchestra. Time and place ceased to matter as he was transported by the sweep of the Ninth Symphony. He could hear it as well as if he were in the concert hall — the thrilling, uplifting swell of the violins, followed by the deep, powerful French horns. The slower, melodic movements gave way, after several long minutes, to a gradual building of the music. Then it soared upward, paused, repeated, swept onward again, surging, intertwining rivers of sound, bringing the familiar theme at last to a crashing crescendo. He heard once more the roar of applause as the crowd in the concert hall rose to their feet in appreciation.

Slowly the vision faded, leaving an aftertaste of satisfaction. He sat up and stretched. The grass was still rippling in quiet waves all around him. Natural beauty and man-made beauty — the best of both worlds, he thought, getting to his feet and slinging the canteen over his shoulder. He replaced his hat and started down toward his horse to continue his journey, refreshed and relaxed.

Coyle traveled two more days without seeing another human. The solitude was a much-needed time for healing and reflection. He didn't really expect to meet anyone once he entered the broken hills of the Badlands, but still took care to remain inconspicuous. Although he hated to make any noise, he was forced to shoot a rabbit with his rifle to supplement his meager supply of food. Nevertheless, by the time his horse trotted up among the first pines along the southern edge of the

Black Hills, his stomach was flat, and he'd become toughened to the saddle and to sleeping in his bedroll on the ground.

The Sioux had only recently been forced by treaty to give up their sacred Black Hills to the whites. It was an after-the-fact concession since the Black Hills were already swarming with white prospectors and town builders whom the Army allegedly could not keep out. Even though the Sioux used the area only for hunting and religious purposes, Coyle was still somewhat apprehensive as he rode along the bottom of a gulch, following a creek. He felt closed-in as he eyed the steeply rising pine forest on both sides of the gulch. Reason told him ambush was very unlikely, but his nerves were on edge, nonetheless. He took a deep breath of the fresh pine-scented air, and tried to relax, to think ahead. If he was to be uneasy about anything, he told himself, he should be wary of encountering white civilization again in Deadwood. The town was only a few months old, and already he'd heard rumors of a roaring boom town — a raw, mud-and-manure, tree stump, shack-and-tent hell hole along the bottom of a gulch where every other building was a saloon. It was a place, he was told by eyewitnesses not given to hyperbole, where men gambled, robbed, whored, and killed each other twenty-four hours a day, and

46

gold dust flowed like fine sand onto bars and balance scales — where life and morals were held in equally low esteem. The force of law, he knew, always followed these boom towns, but at a distance of time. He wasn't sure just how he'd react when he reached Deadwood. In fact, he wasn't even sure exactly where the settlement was located. Northern part of the Black Hills was all he'd been told. So far, he'd struck no road, although he knew a stagecoach was already making regular runs between Deadwood and Cheyenne and also to the new town of Rapid City, on the plains just to the east of the Black Hills.

Although it was nearly the longest day of the year, the sun disappeared early, blocked by trees and hills. It was just as well, since both Coyle and his horse were feeling the effects of several days of hard travel, and he decided to find a good campsite before darkness closed down. There was no shortage of good water. The creek he followed ran clear and cold over a gravelly bottom. He found a level spot, backed by a steep, tree-covered slope, and set up camp, unsaddling and hobbling his horse, collecting a few small pieces of dry driftwood for a fire. He hunkered down close to the fire to ward off the chill that began settling in quickly as soon as the sun was gone. He had nothing to cook; the fire was only for light and warmth. He carried no grain for his horse that had subsisted on grass since leaving Omaha, except for a feed of oats he'd obtained on a stop at Fort Hartsuff. But if Indian ponies could thrive on grass, so could this horse. If there was any grain available in Deadwood, he was sure it would be expensive.

He sat by the fire, listening to the gentle gurgling of the creek and the sounds of his horse ripping up mouthfuls of luxuriant grass nearby. He spread his oiled canvas ground cloth and sat on it, staring into the flames. It was too early to roll into his blanket and go to sleep, even though he was dull with fatigue. He was sure some of this was from lack of proper food, but he felt no hunger pangs. Just as well, since all he had was cold creek water. Earlier that day he'd glimpsed three groups totaling about a dozen miners, panning the creek. Perhaps it was reluctance to establish human contact again, but he'd detoured around them and ridden past without stopping or speaking. He had no reason to stop, except maybe to beg food. He justified his avoidance by reasoning that these prospectors would be wary of any strangers since so many armed men were roaming the hills.

As he sat, staring into the fire with only his horse for company, a sense of loneliness stole over him. The pain he'd been repressing for several days since the court-martial now crept in to surround him like the encircling darkness. In spite of his resolve to block these things from his mind, he began going over the events of the past two months, examining in detail his own actions, trying to find a decision he would make differently if he had it to do over again. It provided some satisfaction to realize that he would not have changed a thing. Much of what had transpired he could not control.

Finally, as the fire burned down, he stood and shook out his blanket, and swung it around his shoulders to ward off the chill. Fatigue was allowing pain and regrets to seem insurmountable. Time, he thought, to "knit up the raveled sleeve of care," as Shakespeare described the benefits of a good sleep.

The sun was not yet up when he awoke, and a light fog hung over the windless gulch. His blanket was drenched with dew, as Coyle stood and shivered himself awake. He walked downstream from his camp and urinated, from force of habit stepping behind a tree to do so. There were no hot coals under the dead ashes of his campfire. Maybe he would just forget the fire and push on, taking a long drink from his canteen. But he was in no hurry and wanted to drive some warmth into his bones and dry his blanket and ground cover before rolling them behind his saddle. He swung his gun belt on and buckled it. The thick mats of fallen pine needles up under the trees would provide some dry tinder, he thought, climbing up the slope. He scooped up several handfuls of dry pine needles and stuffed them into the side pockets of his jacket. "Now for some dead limbs," he muttered, digging his boots into the bank and pushing upward toward a fallen pine that contained all the dry fuel he needed.

While in the process of breaking off some dry twigs, Coyle's glance fell on something red in the green surroundings. He straightened, his pulse beginning to quicken, his senses suddenly alert. It was a narrow strip of red cloth hanging in a tree about thirty yards away. He moved toward it, looking carefully around, listening for any unusual sounds. As he approached, he saw a platform, like a tree house, about ten feet off the ground in the fork of a gnarled oak. But it was not a child's tree house, he realized, as he stopped and stared upward. There was a bundle resting on the platform, and he recognized it as an Indian tree burial. The body had been tightly wrapped and bound in hides. The whole thing was considerably weathered and deteriorated, with several pieces of the rotted hide dangling from the bundle. The platform was sagging. How long the corpse had been here, he could only guess. At least ten years, he thought. By standing back a few feet, he thought he could detect one end of a lance and maybe a curve of a shield that had been placed with the body. Probably a warrior, he concluded. And the wispy remains of a horse's tail still dangled from one corner of the platform. His favorite horse had probably been killed and placed nearby as well, although no trace of the animal was now to be seen. The whole thing presented an aspect of age and decay, except the strip of red cloth, which was very new. Tree burials and scaffold burials were common to the plains Indians, he knew, but to which tribe this belonged he couldn't tell. Probably Sioux or Blackfoot, this far north.

He walked up and touched the strip of red cloth. It was not faded or water-stained. It was not even wet from this morning's dew. The significance of this dawned on him as he felt a chill and put a hand to his gun.

"Don't touch it," a voice spoke, not thirty feet from him.

Coyle gasped and jumped back behind a tree, pulling his pistol. His eyes searched wildly for the source of the voice.

"I have a rifle pointed at you," the voice

51

said. "If you are a grave robber, you will not leave here alive." The voice was soft, yet enunciated the words very clearly. "Put your gun away," it instructed.

Coyle re-holstered his Colt. "I wasn't going to rob it. Only curious," he managed to articulate. His own voice sounded strained. The small pine he stood behind shielded only half of his body.

The light was strengthening as the sun topped a hill, its rays striking the tall treetops, making the dew sparkle like millions of tiny glass fragments. He still could not see the speaker.

A figure glided noiselessly from the cover of a thick pine, holding a Winchester at waist level. It was a very lean Indian with slightly hooded eyes and black hair pulled back into a ponytail. He was shorter than Coyle's five-foot, ten inches, and wore a pair of canvas pants and a plaid shirt. The only item of native apparel was his thick-soled moccasins decorated with a tiny bit of green beadwork.

Coyle encompassed all these details at a glance. "I would never desecrate a grave . . . Indian or white," he said.

"What are you doing here?"

"I'm on my way to Deadwood. Just gathering wood for a campfire and stumbled onto this," he added.

"There's nothing of value here," the Indian said, motioning him back with the rifle. "Get your firewood and leave."

Coyle silently bent to the task of gathering up the dry sticks he'd dropped. He sneaked a glance at the man's face. Was that a look of malevolence, or just grim seriousness?

"A relative of yours?" Coyle asked to break the tension as he continued searching for dead sticks.

"My father."

"I'm sorry."

"No need to be. He's been dead thirteen years. I pay homage to him every trip I make to the hills."

Coyle wondered about the status of an Indian who spoke careful, boarding-school English and dressed in white man's clothing.

"Are you Sioux?"

"Lakota," the Indian corrected him.

"The Lakota believe in an afterlife," Coyle remarked.

"Of course. But I'm Presbyterian now," he stated matter-of-factly. "Thinking of switching to the Catholics or Episcopalians. The Presbyterians can't quite convince me that it's already determined where we go after we die. If it's already decided, why live?"

"If you're Christian, why the tree burial for your father?" Coyle asked, curiosity getting the better of his earlier fright.

The Indian had lowered the rifle, but still kept his distance. "He died when I was only seventeen and still believed in the old ways. My mother and uncles helped with the burial here, as befitting a great warrior of the Miniconjous. We never thought he'd be disturbed," he added pointedly. "But now the hills are overrun by white men crazy for gold, scaring off the game and cutting down the timber to build their damn' towns." His voice was edged with bitterness. "But my father's spirit has gone to his ancestors. Tree burials are cleaner, more in tune with nature. His body is being absorbed by the elements, back to where it came from."

"I've always had a fear of being put into a hole in the ground myself," Coyle remarked, straightening up with an armful of dead sticks. He looked closer at the Lakota who didn't seem to be much of a threat now. The dates the man had given would make him about thirty. "What's your name?"

"Tom Merritt."

"Your Indian name?"

"Swift Hawk." His was almost a sad smile. "A little more noble and elegant, wouldn't you say?"

Coyle nodded.

"But it won't get me anywhere in your

world. I just took that Tom Merritt from a character in a book after I learned to read."

"Doesn't really matter what a man calls himself. I'm Thad Coyle, but I didn't pick either of those names."

Merritt nodded. "I have your promise you won't touch this burial site?"

"You have it."

He grunted affirmatively and swung the rifle into the crook of his arm. "I have to get back to my wagon and team. The sun's nearly over the hills."

"Where are you going?"

"Deadwood. I run a freight wagon. Bring supplies from the railroad at Rushville, and sometimes Valentine. Have to make money while I can."

If this man had a wagon, there had to be a road nearby. "Swift Hawk, I'm going to Deadwood, but I don't know the way. Mind if I fetch my horse and ride along with you?"

The slender Indian hesitated. "As long as you don't call me Swift Hawk."

Coyle thought he detected a trace of a smile as the man turned away.

Chapter Three

June 22, 1876
Denison, Iowa

Emma Coyle put down the past Sunday's edition of *The Des Moines Register* and looked across the room at her daughter Jill, who had fallen asleep on the horsehair sofa. The four-year old, who protested that she was a big girl now and didn't need a nap, had worn herself out playing tag and jump rope with some of her new friends in the neighborhood and involuntarily dozed off just after lunch.

Emma looked at the blonde hair fallen across the child's face as she slept and noticed the slight summer breeze stirring the white curtains near the sofa. Emma didn't want to risk waking her by slipping off Jill's shoes. She knew her mother, Arminta Douglas, would be harshly critical of shoes on the good furniture, but Arminta was at the dry goods store she'd inherited from Emma's father, preparing to put the store up for sale. Emma didn't know what her mother planned to do with the money or her life, once the store was sold, but she assumed Arminta would confide in her when the time came.

Bradley was out playing cowboys and Indians with two older neighborhood boys he'd just met. She was glad there were other children who lived nearby, since it was summer vacation, and without the contacts at school her son would have little chance to meet and make new friends.

Emma got to her feet and paced to the window, unbuttoning the neck of her dress and fanning herself with part of the newspaper. It was certainly warm and muggy. A bakery wagon passed down the street, the horse's hoofs *clopping* loudly on the hard-packed street beyond the iron picket fence that enclosed the yard. Compared to Omaha or Council Bluffs, this small town was quiet to the point of boredom. She and the children had been here only two weeks, but she was already feeling discontented. In fact, she'd sensed something amiss the first day or two after she'd arrived. Her parents had moved here just after Emma had married so she had no childhood memories of this house or this town. Although her widowed mother had indicated the three of them were most welcome here, Emma knew her mother had some reservations about taking her back home with the disgrace hanging over Emma's separated, non-supporting husband. Emma wasn't sure if her mother blamed her for the trouble, or blamed Thaddeus, as she insisted on calling him. Emma had done everything she could think of to fit in and please her mother since their arrival. But Arminta, although she gave lip service to welcoming them, seemed to remain somewhat aloof. Emma worked hard, keeping the house clean, helping prepare the meals, and especially trying to keep the children from aggravating their grandmother. Arminta's ideas of disciplining children were rather harsh. Maybe it was because she had not been around small children for a number of years.

Emma's offer to help inventory the store's goods preparatory to the sale had been declined. Arminta said she had two clerks to help and had strongly suggested that Emma stay home, do the housework, and look after the children. She had plenty of experience doing both, Emma thought with some vexation. For some reason she was slightly depressed. Maybe she'd expected something different — a new beginning perhaps. Even though she had no thought of creating even more scandal by divorcing Thad, she could not look forward to receiving the small, but steady, allotment he'd always sent from his military pay. Of necessity, she'd been concerned mostly with finances, trying to keep her children and herself in clothing and food and shelter, juggling bills, stalling the grocer, gladly accepting hand-me-downs of clothing from friends whose children had outgrown them. She'd become an expert at cutting corners until it was now an ingrained habit. If suddenly she had all the money she wanted, would this parsimony continue? Being here so far had not provided her the secure comfort she'd expected. Emma was beginning to feel the loss of her own independence and having any of her own money.

As she crossed the room toward the kitchen, she caught sight of herself in the big oval mirror on the hall closet door. She paused and examined the image, surprised by the frown on her face. The sharp nose, the down-turned mouth, the brown hair piled atop her head — they all reminded her of a waspish schoolteacher she'd had as a little girl. "Lord, I hope I'm not getting like that," she muttered aloud. In spite of having borne two children, her figure remained good, even without the hot, binding corset. Overall still an attractive woman, she decided, if she could cultivate a happier attitude, that would show through. She was afraid she was going down the road her mother had taken, eventually becoming an aging shrew to whom nothing was pleasing or humorous.

Maybe it was the loss of the men in their lives that accounted for the imbalance, she thought as she went on into the kitchen. The house seemed so different with her father gone. His presence still seemed to permeate the place, from the magazine rack by his favorite chair, to the aura of old cigar smoke that still clung to the upholstered furniture. It was almost as if he were in the next room and might walk in at any moment. He'd been a strong man, barrel-chested and bearded, a natty dresser. It was hard to reconcile her mind to the fact that she would never see him again. He'd been dead these past ten months.

Her father — how unlike her husband! Thad was much less outgoing, less demonstrative. She and Thad had not communicated as well as they might have — as well as they should have. She tried to analyze her feelings for Thad while she absently began gathering the ingredients to roll out two pie crusts. She and Thad had lived apart off and on for most of their nine years of marriage, interspersed with a week here or a month there of his leave at home when they'd enjoyed each other's company. They'd not had time to grow tired of one another, or to find out how little they had in common. Her shabby surroundings in rented rooms and boarding houses had not seemed to bother him. Money, or the lack thereof, was something that didn't enter his mind. He was the dreamer, the idealist, not concerned with the here and now. He rarely got upset about anything, but neither was he a leader. He seemed content just to drift along with no goals, and let his family do the same. He had not pushed for his own promotions in the Army, did not play politics, or curry favor with his superiors.

She assembled the flour, salt, yeast, bread board, rolling pin, and bowls, then slipped an apron over her head and tied the strings behind. She opened the left-hand door of the cook stove and pitched in a double handful of dry corn cobs, followed by several sticks of split oak from the wood box. She sloshed in some coal oil and struck a match to it, closing the door. If only she'd had a kitchen like this of her own to work in, or was she unduly concerned with material things, she wondered as she pumped some water into the sink and washed her hands. Well, one of them had to be practical, she thought. Thad certainly wasn't. But did that make him any worse a man and husband? She had loved him at one time. He was kind and had a way of treating her that made her feel special. She felt a twinge of regret at taking an almost savage delight in blaming him for the whole débâcle of his court-martial. She recalled the crushed look on his face when it paled under the shadow of his clean-shaven cheeks. God! Maybe she *was* becoming more like her mother — judgmental and overly critical. Did she still love Thad? It was a question that came to her most often at night when she was tired. At this point she could not answer it. But there was an undefined ache in her heart, day and night, a longing for something, she didn't know what.

The children missed him and continued to ask when he was coming home, even though she gave them only vague answers. Children, by nature, were trusting and accepted without question the living arrangements. They had taken eagerly to their new surroundings. Where was Thad now? He'd mentioned going West to the gold fields, but was rather indefinite about his plans.

She sighed, opening the oven door to check the heat of the fire, thinking there was no such fire within her own breast. She was not passionate about anything, and pictured herself several years from now a shriveled shrew, full of venom, sniping at everyone and everything — and shuddered at the vision. She had to make something positive of her life, and had to start soon.

She worked out her frustration with a hard,

physical kneading of the bread dough on the board, finally shaping it into two loaves in the pans and setting them aside to rise. Then she rolled out two pie crusts, fit them to the circular pans, and filled them with the dried apples she'd been soaking, adding cinnamon, brown sugar, and a pinch of salt and nutmeg along with a few slices of green tomato for tartness. She placed lids on the crusts, pinched the edges all around, poked air holes in each, and set the pans carefully in the oven.

Perspiring, she wiped her damp face and hands with a towel, then stepped out into the back yard to escape the heat of the kitchen and to check the sheets on the clothesline.

"Emma! How are you this fine day?" Margot Connor, the neighbor behind them, came over and leaned on the low, wooden fence, the sun gleaming on her silver hair, her round face beaming.

"I'm doing well, Missus Connor."

"Call me Margot. Remember?"

Emma was hardly in the mood for the perpetual cheerfulness of this woman, but nodded politely.

"Will you and the children be staying on, then?"

"I'm not sure what our plans will be. We'll probably be here for a few months yet. Possibly through summer. I want to get Bradley into school."

"I'll be glad to have good neighbors after Arminta leaves."

Startled, Emma turned from the damp sheets. "After Mother leaves?"

"Oh, dear!" Mrs. Connor looked flustered. "She hasn't told you, then?"

"Told me what?"

"Maybe you should ask *her*."

"Tell me." Emma couldn't keep the peevishness out of her voice.

Mrs. Connor looked distressed, but replied: "Arminta told me she's going to marry that Mormon she's been seeing. Going to join the Latter-Day Saints and move to Utah."

Emma felt her heart skip a beat. She had trouble getting her breath, but tried to calm herself. "She told you that?"

"With her own mouth." Worry lines creased Mrs. Connor's forehead between the eyebrows. "He's a rich man, to be sure, but it's not natural."

"Natural?" Emma repeated, stunned.

"Well, him having two wives already and all. But, I suppose a woman Arminta's age should be grateful to get a man at all."

Emma felt as if someone had just struck her squarely between the eyes with a stick of cordwood. More than likely, this Mormon,

64

whoever he was, had his eye on the profit from the sale of her mother's store. Emma turned away without another word and stumbled numbly back into the house.

Chapter Four

June 18, 1876
Deadwood, Dakota Territory

Thad Coyle's first impression was one of astonishment when he and Tom Merritt rode down the main street of Deadwood. Even though he'd heard tales of the place, the reality of it jarred his sensibilities. After years of military life where post buildings and barracks were properly cleaned and maintained, where discipline and routine were the order of the day, Deadwood was somewhat unnerving. Uneven rows of shacks and tents were divided by a street that was a quagmire of black mud from recent rains churned up by thousands of hoofs and wheels. A teamster, whose wagon was hub-deep and blocking traffic, was being roundly cursed by others trying to get past. The teamster was dividing his time between cursing the straining mules and cursing the men who were shouting at him.

Coyle and the Indian went their separate ways, and Coyle dismounted near one of many saloons that lined the street. As he tied his horse to the hitching rail, he noted the flood of sunshine in the bottom of the narrow gulch — a consequence of the deforestation all around where trees had been harvested to build the town. A forest of stumps now covered the hillsides.

The lone bartender inside was too busy waiting on the midday customers to be bothered answering questions about the town or the prospects of gold or anything else. Coyle shoved into the noisy, jostling crowd by the plank bar until he'd worked himself up close enough to signal above the din for a beer. Although his stomach was grumbling, food, for the moment, was out of the question.

Standing up in a corner to avoid the crush, he finished his beer, then pushed out through the batwing doors into the welcome fresh air of the street. He left his horse for the moment and walked down the street until he found a combination restaurant/saloon a few doors away that wasn't as crowded. Cringing at the high prices, he spent his last three dollars on a hearty meal of venison stew and homemade bread.

"What're the chances of a job in this town?" he inquired of the waiter who brought his food.

"Hell, mister, just look around you!" the

aproned man said, waving his arm. "You can take your pick of jobs. Everybody's begging for help. Most men who come through here are in a sweat to be off to the creeks to scoop up their fortunes. Judging from the number I've seen coming back out of the hills and selling their outfits, a man would be better off gettin' hisself a job and rakin' in the dust while this boom lasts. Ain't no higher wages in the country, I'm thinkin' . . . even for common labor."

"Thanks for the advice."

"You betcha."

Coyle, in need of immediate cash, applied at the first HELP WANTED sign he saw and immediately secured a job as a lowly swamper in the Nugget Saloon. The wages were higher than he expected, but lodging was practically non-existent, he discovered, in a town that was struggling mightily to create itself, but lagging behind the demands of the new population. The owner of the Nugget allowed him to sleep on the floor in his back room and tether his horse out back in the weather. Even if he could have afforded it, the livery stable was full to overflowing and every newcomer was clamoring for space for his animals.

When he started this job, he had nothing but the dirty clothes he wore, his guns, horse, and saddle. He wasn't about to part with any of these for a grubstake and miner's pan and shovel. With everyone heading for the creeks, there was a crying need for skilled and unskilled workers. After a week of sweeping, mopping, trimming wicks and filling lamps, dumping trash and cleaning cuspidors, Coyle drew his pay and took a better-paying job as a carpenter's helper. Buildings were going up everywhere, and the new sawmill was one of the busiest places in the gulch. Powered at first by water, then by a steam engine, the mill turned out millions of board feet of green pine lumber. From daylight to dark, the air was filled with the staccato rapping of hammers and the whining and screeching of the circular saws. The fresh scent of pine sap even overrode the stench of manure and privies that pervaded the town.

If there was more than placer gold in these granite hills, hard-rock mining would surely follow, he thought. Heavy machinery would eventually replace the pan and shovel, and men on wages would work in shifts around the clock. But now, when twilight closed down and lamps flared up and down Main Street, the population set itself to play as hard as it had worked. Drunken arguments broke out in the street, some of which ended with blasts of gunfire. Bartenders with shotguns tried to keep a semblance of order in their establishments.

Coyle avoided most of this hellish night life, usually so tired that he sought his bedroll in the back of an unfinished building he was helping construct.

One afternoon, eleven days after arriving in town, Coyle was sitting on a keg of nails, smoking his pipe, when he noticed an Indian loping up the street, weaving in and out of the foot traffic. His long black hair was stringy and his hide vest plastered to his chest by sweat. As the runner passed, Coyle saw that the lean Indian was laboring in the throes of extreme exhaustion. He thought the man's rubbery legs were going to give out before he staggered into the office of the *Deadwood Sentinal.*

It was only minutes before the incredible news was spreading along the street like a wind-driven fire. Custer and all his men were dead at the hands of a band of the Sioux and Northern Cheyennes! How did such a wild story as that get started? An Indian brought word, you say? What Indian? Some place in Montana? Men abandoned their poker games and carried their drinks outside. Workers climbed off roofs, wiping sweat, gathered around water barrels, drinking from dippers and discussing the shocking tale brought by this Indian runner. Good-time girls leaned out of upstairs windows, watching.

The editor of the *Sentinal* was apparently convinced the message was true, since he had a special edition out on the street within an hour. Men passed copies of the one-page paper from hand to hand before the ink was even dry. Copies were tacked up on wooden store fronts, and the crowds jostled to get a look at the story that gave more details. In bits and pieces, Coyle got the story of the massacre. Many of the men on the street loudly condemned the news as a complete hoax, but Coyle had an instinctive feeling it was true. Among Army officers, Custer always had a reputation as an arrogant, lucky fool. Even if Coyle had still been on active duty, he would not have been with the 7th cavalry on those upland slopes above the Little Big Horn River that Sunday. But he knew he could very well have met his own death on the sandhills of Nebraska only two months ago, or before, during the war. He was beginning to see that his leaving the service, even under dishonorable conditions, was a blessing in the perspective of the rest of his life. Man did not control his own destiny, he thought, fingering the torn newspaper he held. He only reacted to situations. He took the cold pipe from the corner of his mouth and knocked the dottle out of the bowl against the side of a building.

71

Then, for some reason feeling vulnerable and uneasy, he walked off alone down the street.

It was his chance meeting with the poet/scout Jack Crawford that jarred Coyle out of his comfortable groove in Deadwood in September of 1876. Coyle, with a penchant for order, had naturally gravitated to a job with steady hours and regular pay, and had clung to it for three months while the more transient population of gold seekers seethed around him.

He first saw Crawford on the main street of Deadwood — a handsome six-footer with shoulder-length hair, mustache, and goatee, wearing a fringed buckskin jacket and holstered pistols. Coyle stopped to stare, since the man, from a distance, looked like a reincarnation of James Butler "Wild Bill" Hickok who had been gunned down in a local saloon six weeks earlier. As the apparition came closer, he looked more like Buffalo Bill Cody, who was presently touring with his new Wild West show.

The man saw Coyle staring and paused. "Howdy! Do I know you?"

Coyle shook his head.

"Name's Jack Crawford." He thrust out his hand.

At the time, the name meant nothing to

Coyle. Just someone trying to look like a mountain man or the more famous scout, Cody. Up close, the man appeared gaunt and hollow-eyed, but he had a strong grip.

"I'm Thaddeus Coyle." He shook hands briefly. He had no reason to make this man's acquaintance and turned to pass on down the street.

"Have you seen the story of General Crook's battle at Slim Buttes?" Crawford asked, thrusting a copy of the *Deadwood Sentinel* into his hands. As Coyle glanced at it, Crawford yelled at a newsboy nearby and bought himself another copy.

Coyle scanned the front-page article that apparently detailed the story of the summer-long pursuit of the Sioux after the Custer fight. "Uh . . . thanks. I'll read it," he said, trying to concoct some excuse to slide away without being rude. "Here's a nickel for the paper."

Crawford waved it off. "They didn't give me a by-line on this, but James Gordon Bennett of the *New York Herald* paid me over five hundred dollars for that story. The *Sentinal* reprinted a condensed version of it."

Coyle glanced at him with renewed curiosity. "I would never have taken you for a reporter."

"I write poetry mostly. But I was scouting

for Crook and experienced the whole march and the battle first-hand. Killed a horse trying to beat the other scout, Frank Grouard, to the nearest telegraph office at Fort Laramie to file my story first."

Coyle was intrigued. "Come on. If you've got a minute, I'd like to buy you a drink. You can give me your behind-the-scene story."

"I don't drink."

"How about a steak, then?" Coyle suggested, eyeing his gaunt appearance. "Unless you're a vegetarian, too."

"Been a long time since I had a steak. You're on." The scout had an infectious grin.

Coyle detected a trace of an accent. "Where you from?" he asked as the two crossed the street toward an eating establishment that advertised both beef and antelope steaks.

"Born in Ireland, I'm proud to say. My parents brought me to this heavenly country during the Great Hunger. They dallied a bit on the way, and I think my young brain was starved for nourishment. Maybe that's why I'm still a bit daft." He smiled and touched the side of his head.

During the next two hours, Coyle discovered that Jack Crawford was one of those gregarious individuals who literally never met a stranger. He appeared to be about Coyle's age — mid-thirties.

The scout put away a steak and fried potatoes, sopping up the juice with large hunks of homemade bread torn from a loaf in the middle of the table. But his eating never slowed his tongue as he spun out the yarn of the summer-long march in almost continuous rain and mud from southern Montana into the Dakota Territory in pursuit of the Sioux who had annihilated Custer and his troop. He related the suffering of the soldiers as Crook's command ran out of food and were forced to shoot and eat their dying horses and mules. The men were calling it the "starvation march," and the "horse-meat march." Crook was adamant that they not give up the pursuit and turn south to the Black Hills for supplies.

"Well, his persistence finally paid off," Crawford continued. "We caught up with them some miles north of here at a park-like place the Indians call Slim Buttes. Fog and rain so thick we couldn't see what we were firing at."

"So you took them prisoner?"

"Killed a bunch first who wanted to fight. But we captured most of them. A few got away. Found some trophies they'd taken from the dead troopers of Custer's Seventh." He took a swig of coffee. "Worst expedition I've ever been on," Crawford concluded with uncharacteristic seriousness, as he forked in some more potatoes. "I think I'm done with scouting."

"You said you're a poet besides being a reporter?"

"You might say that," he grinned, wiping his mouth. "I'm glad you mentioned that. Here's one I didn't have a chance to get into the newspaper earlier." He pulled a paper from his pocket and unfolded it. "This is for Wild Bill, a fellow scout. I wasn't here when he was shot down, but the news hit me hard. Here's a tribute to him."

> Sleep on brave heart, in peaceful
>   slumber,
> Bravest scout in all the West;
> Lightning eyes and voice of thunder,
> Closed and hushed in quiet rest.
> Peace and rest at last is given,
> May we meet again in heaven.
> Rest in peace.

"Very nice," Coyle remarked, secretly dismissing the verse as sentimental rubbish. But that kind of thing was popular and drew a tear to the eye of many a miner. While Coyle was digesting the verse, his irrepressible tablemate was already off to another topic.

"Poetry and scouting aren't my only talents," he said. "I can sing, too."

76

Before Coyle could deter him, Crawford launched into a rendition of "Mother McCree." Conversations stopped at other tables, and heads turned in their direction. Coyle could feel his own face reddening with embarrassment. Coyle had never seen a sober man who could, or would, burst into a song in public like this. Crawford had a fine tenor voice, and he was not the least bit self-conscious about singing for his supper. Apparently any place was his stage, and he was bent on enjoying himself.

Crawford finished his song and leaned back in his chair, crossing one booted leg over the other. "I'm a little out of voice. A touch of catarrh I picked up in the fog and wet on that horse-meat march."

The other patrons had gone back to their own conversations. Coyle was pleasantly stuffed and decided not to go for the dried apple pie.

"Have you struck a good pocket or some placer gold?" Crawford asked matter-of-factly.

"I've never been prospecting," Coyle replied, somewhat surprised.

"Really? I thought everybody in this town was after gold. I can hardly wait to get out and try my luck. And I'm looking for a partner. Why don't you join me?"

77

Coyle didn't reply for several seconds. He'd earned a decent stake since he'd been working, but he'd also started promising himself that he was going to take the plunge, throw off his cautious ways, and give lady luck a whirl. It was against his nature, but he wanted a clean break with the past. Yet, here he was, three months later, still drawing regular pay.

"Hell, yes. I'll join up with you!" he heard himself saying to this stranger. "I can't wait to get to the creeks before winter closes in."

For the first two weeks they found only enough traces of placer gold to encourage them to file a claim on Deadwood Creek about five miles from town. But, after a month, they discovered why this particular stretch of creek was not already staked. It yielded only enough gold to keep their interest and to meet minimal expenses. The best thing about this partnership was Crawford's perpetual good nature and willingness to do more than his share of the work. The two of them got along famously even when Coyle was more than a little morose about their lack of good fortune. It was around the campfire at night that Crawford was worth more than any wages he could have been paid. He had the capacity to tell stories by the hour, recite epic poems with dramatic effect, and knew the words to dozens of songs, often accompanying himself on a mandolin. Coyle found himself wishing he'd had this man for a scout on active duty.

As mid-October came and went, ice began to appear along the edges of the quieter stretches of the stream each morning. Wading knee-deep in the icy water was a numbing experience each of them could stand for only about twenty minutes. They took to keeping a fire burning all the time to warm up quickly as they relieved each other, one working the rocker and one shoveling the gravel.

"Jack, this just isn't working," Coyle finally said late one afternoon as darkness forced a halt to the daily operation.

"It was a long shot," Crawford replied cheerfully, jamming the shovel into the gravel bar. "But I had to try, anyway. Couldn't leave the hills without at least testing my luck."

By mutual consent, they abandoned their claim and tried three other sites farther upstream in the next week, with even less to show for their efforts. By then, early November was putting a chill on their enthusiasm. Except for two trips to Deadwood for supplies, they'd seen only a half dozen prospectors passing their camp, nurturing their own dreams of bonanza.

"Believe we got here a little late," Crawford

said one evening, sitting cross-legged on the ground cloth and rubbing the chilblains on his lower legs. "If we keep at this, we'd better start thinking of some kind of permanent shelter for winter."

Coyle nodded, handing Crawford a smoking plate of bacon and beans. It was a necessity he'd been considering for some time.

They ate in silence for several minutes, listening to the crackle of the fire and the rushing of nearby Deadwood Creek.

"Pardner, I think I've had just about enough prospecting," Crawford finally said, setting down his plate. "It's time for me to be moving on to something else. And I believe I can mine this experience in my new occupation."

"And what would that be?"

"Show business."

"You'd be a natural," Coyle agreed.

"Thought I'd see if I could bust into Cody's Wild West show. Sort of get my feet wet that way. He's already got an established reputation and a ready audience."

"What would you be? A marksman? A barker?"

"A frontier Army scout. I'd play myself. Maybe write and recite a little poetry . . . whatever Colonel Cody would have me do."

"Good idea," Coyle said, wondering silently about his own future.

The next morning they packed up their gear and remaining food, leaving the crude rocker in the edge of the stream for someone else to find and use.

Back in town, they sold their shovels and pans. Each had a small, mostly limp, rawhide poke. "I'll have to wash this sack to find the dust in it," Crawford said, as they shook hands. "But it's been a great experience, and I wouldn't trade it for anything. I'll find my gold on the stage."

With hearty good wishes, both men mounted up and rode out of town in opposite directions, Coyle heading southeast for the new town of Rapid City. It was the last he saw of Crawford.

Chapter Five

June, 1877
Railroad Dépôt
Rushville, Nebraska

"Hey, Injun! You forgot one." The beefy freight handler aimed a kick at a small wooden box. The box skidded across the floor of the boxcar and bounced down onto the dépôt platform.

Thad Coyle looked up from securing the canvas cover over a load of freight in the heavy wagon. He watched Tom Merritt step back up onto the platform, scoop up the box, and examine the damage. He snapped the remains of a splinter that had split off part of the stenciled word: FRAGILE.

"Anything broken inside here, the railroad will pay for it," Merritt said.

The stocky man stood in the open door of the boxcar, wiping sweat from his red face and grinning. "The hell you say!"

"My customers expect me to deliver their goods undamaged. I'm responsible," Merritt added.

"Then you better unload this damned freight yourself," the man said.

"That's what you get paid to do," Merritt said, shaking the box gently near his ear.

"I don't need some gaw-damned red nigger telling me what my job is!" the man retorted, vaulting down from the freight car with an agility that belied his bulk. He was flexing his shoulders and shoving shirt sleeves up over massive, hairy forearms. As he moved closer, Coyle could see the tracery of tiny purple veins in the whisky-burned cheeks.

"Back off, mister," Coyle said quietly, sliding in front of Merritt.

The bigger man took a step back and looked Coyle up and down. "This ain't none o' your affair," he sneered. "You better tell your lackey to watch his mouth."

"He's not my lackey. He's my partner," Coyle said.

"Shit! A gaw-damned, scum-suckin' Injun-lover! The lowest form of white man!" he fairly howled.

Coyle's fist slammed flat against the fleshy nose.

The man staggered back, sputtering, blood streaming from his nostrils. "You son-of-a-bitch!" he roared, regaining his balance and wiping a hand across his face. In the second or two it took for him to glance at his reddened hand and decide to charge, Coyle had his Colt out of its holster. He stepped forward to meet the rush and swung the 7½-inch barrel like a short club. The metal cracked against bone, dropping the man to his knees, a gash opened across his forehead. A quick, hard kick to the groin kept him down.

"Let's get out of here." Coyle jerked his head at the two wagons and teams that stood nearby, loaded, hitched, and ready. His heart was pounding as he holstered his gun.

"I don't see any reason to stay," Merritt agreed, springing to the nearest wagon seat.

Coyle, with a last look at the moaning man, followed quickly to the other wagon, whipping the looped lines free of the brake handle. *"Hyah!"* He snapped the reins over the backs of the gray mules, and the wagon lurched into motion. As they pulled out, a quick glance over his shoulder showed him the stationmaster coming out of the dépôt, shotgun in hand. Two porters had dropped what they were doing to come to the aid of the man on the platform. Coyle faced forward and cracked the lines again, urging the mules to a faster pace as they lumbered down the street of Rushville toward the open prairie beyond.

Once the loaded wagons were rolling smoothly over the hard-packed road, they made good time and didn't pause for more than two hours. Then Merritt signaled with his arm and pulled his team off the road. A clump of cottonwoods bordered a small stream. The two men stopped their wagons a few yards apart, letting the thirsty mules move down the low creekbank to water.

Coyle and Merritt paced away a short distance as Merritt reached for the makings in his shirt pocket and began rolling a smoke. Coyle took off his hat and ran a sleeve across his face. "*Whew!* That breeze feels good."

Merritt didn't reply as he licked the cigarette and placed it between his lips. Then he struck a light to his smoke and inhaled deeply. Coyle, watching him, thought his friend smoked far too much. If Merritt's skin hadn't already been dark, his fingers would have shown brown stains.

"You should probably start carrying a weapon," Coyle remarked.

"Because of that fracas back there?" He shook his head.

"What did you do with men like that before you partnered up with me?"

Merritt shrugged. "I handled it one way or another. If I carried a gun, except for that rifle on the wagon, I would be tempted to use it. And that would make trouble for sure. If I ever shot a white man, I'd be hung, regardless of the situation. And if I pulled a pistol, that would be an excuse for someone else to shoot me. No . . ." — he shook his head, taking a small puff on the stubby cigarette — "that's not my way of doing things."

"What about your pride, your self-respect?" Coyle asked.

"That is in here," he replied, tapping his breast. "I don't have to prove it to anyone else."

"Your Indian brothers might call that losing face," Coyle suggested. When Merritt glanced up sharply, Coyle wished he'd kept his mouth shut.

"I don't live by the old ways of the tribe any more. I've learned to function in the white world . . . and have done very well," he added. "Certainly well enough that I needed a partner to expand."

"True enough." Since Coyle had wandered into Rapid City seven months before, looking for work, and had run into Merritt again, the arrangement seemed made to order. Coyle wanted some kind of job that would keep him outdoors most of the time. Over a drink, he had readily accepted Merritt's offer of partnership.

"You know, you and I are two fish out of water," Coyle said after a few moments. "Renegades, outcasts from our own societies. Yours by design and mine by court-martial and an impatient wife."

Merritt nodded. "Men of your race, for the most part, live for money. And that's what I've trained myself to do. But . . . in the long nights, or after a few drinks, sometimes there is an emptiness in my heart."

Coyle looked his curiosity, but waited for him to go on.

"The Lakotas are a free-roaming people but are also tied to the earth. It's not like whites think of land ownership . . . for exclusive use. It's just. . . ." He paused, gesturing helplessly at trying to express the concept. He took one last drag on his cigarette and flipped it away. "It's just that . . . when we are cut off from the land, like many young Lakota men would be if they went to work in the cities, we are cut off from the source of life, like the stem of a plant that has been severed, and we begin to wither. Like this cottonwood, here. . . ." He gestured at the rough-barked giant nearby whose pale leaves were fluttering softly overhead. "If it were somehow ripped up and planted away from this water and sandy soil and sunshine, it would surely die."

"Yet, you've managed," Coyle pointed out.

"I'm stuffing my pockets with gold and greenbacks and putting some into a bank in my name and filling my belly with good beefsteak. But I am slowly starving because my severed stem is in water only, and not in the earth."

"Is that why more young Lakota men don't come off the reservation to work?"

"One of the reasons," Merritt acknowledged. "There are others, just as strong, like the one you saw back there this morning. Not many young bloods of the Lakotas could have endured that without fighting back. They do not all have my temperament."

"So you do what you have to do to get by," Coyle summed up. "You've made your choice to live in a dominant white world, and have to take your beatings."

"Yes. But those on the reservations now have to take their punishments, too, and they lack my freedom and money."

"A man must pay the price for whatever he wants most," Coyle said, recalling the words of his friend, Dr. Mecklenburg, shortly before Coyle had been court-martialed.

Several seconds of silence followed. Coyle became aware of the drowsy hum of bees in the prairie flowers. The mules flicked their long ears at the pestering flies.

"If your people are nomadic, how are they tied to the land?" Coyle asked, breaking the quiet.

"We are tied to the land because it furnishes everything we need to live, such as animals and water and plants for medicine and food. And, when we die, our bodies fall back to dust to mingle with that of the earth. We don't have to cultivate crops or live on one spot of land to feel this kinship with the earth."

"I see."

"Men are linked to all other living things . . . the animals and birds and insects who depend on one another for life, just as we all depend on the renewing cycles of grass and trees and rain."

Coyle stooped, picked up a small stone, and skipped it across the flat surface of the slow-flowing stream. The ripples spread out in silent, overlapping circles. Then he asked the question that had been foremost in his mind since he'd first met Merritt at the tree burial site in the Black Hills. "Why did you decide to leave your people and live in a world you knew would be hostile to you?"

"Don't you think the world is now hostile to my people on the reservations?" he asked, turning to face Coyle. "I saw what was coming to them . . . the poverty, the shame, the restrictions on their lives and movements. I was taught in the boarding school to speak English very well, and I wanted freedom to come and go and do as I pleased, even if it was in an alien culture."

"You dress like a white man, and you changed your name from Swift Hawk to Tom Merritt," Coyle said, "but you still wear your hair long." Now that he had broken through Merritt's quiet reserve, Coyle wanted to push a little further.

"It's obvious that I'm an Indian, so I'm not trying to hide it by dressing white. This is the only type of clothing easily available. As for the hair, I just happen to prefer it long. It was very hard at first. But I kept my eyes down and worked at many menial jobs and made no trouble. I had to live like a beast, but I managed to put away enough money in two years to buy an old wagon and a team of spavined horses. Even though I had a reputation for honesty, I didn't get enough business at first. Then the boom hit the Black Hills, and I had more work at good pay than I could manage. That's when you came along." His weathered features relaxed into as much of a smile as Coyle had ever seen on his face.

The mules turned the wagons slightly as they sidled out into the sunshine, ripping up mouthfuls of grass.

"Ever have any regrets and wish you could go back?"

Merritt shook his head. "My people are doomed unless they jump into this new world like I did. I hate to see them treated like a conquered people in slavery, like the Israelites in Egypt, but that's what they are."

"Then you don't see yourself as Moses, leading them out of bondage?"

Merritt shook his head. "Even Moses required a lot of Divine intervention to accomplish that. And I haven't noticed the Almighty offering to help the Lakotas. They'll only be able to help themselves as individuals. Yet, if enough of them left the reservation and eventually intermarried with other races, I can foresee a time in the future when the Lakotas would disappear as a separate people."

"That would be a sad thing."

Merritt shrugged, moving toward one of the wagons and preparing to climb up. "Everything in the world moves in cycles. If that is to be, then I am powerless to stop it."

Chapter Six

July 19, 1880
Denison, Iowa

Coyle knew something was amiss as soon as he reined up his bay in front of his mother-in-law's house. An old man was rocking on the front porch, smoking his pipe.

Coyle dismounted and tied the reins to a ring in an iron hitching post formed in the shape of a horse's head. He'd been in the saddle far too long these past four days, and walked stiffly as he opened the gate in the iron picket fence and approached the porch.

"Howdy."

"Hello," the white-haired man nodded.

"I'm looking for Emma Coyle. I believe this is her mother's house."

"Don't recognize the name," the old man said, leaning forward with both elbows on his knees. "We bought this house from a Missus Arminta Douglas."

"That's her . . . my mother-in-law," Coyle said, his heart sinking. "Where did she go?"

"She was bustin' a garter to marry a Mormon and move to Utah last I saw of her," the old man replied, light blue eyes looking over his spectacles.

Coyle absorbed this without comment. The old lady had always been a little peculiar in his view, but marrying a Mormon surprised him. "Was there a younger woman and two small children with her?" he asked.

"Can't rightly say. My wife and I moved here from Council Bluffs. We bought this house through a bank nearly two years ago. Only met the old lady once, and she was here by herself the day we come to look the place over."

"Two years ago?" He had trouble keeping the despair out of his voice. He put a foot up on the second porch step and leaned toward the old man who was still seated in the rocker above him. "How do you know she married a Mormon?" he asked, grasping at any scraps of information.

The old man chuckled and spat off the porch into the grass before taking a draw on his pipe. "If it warn't for gossipy neighbors, we'd all keep our own secrets, now, wouldn't we?"

After pumping the old man for any further details, Coyle left and went to the bank that had sold the house. They could give little information, except to say that the owner,

Arminta Douglas, had allowed the bank to collect a commission for advertising and selling both her store and her home. The bank officer said that in a small town most people were aware that Mrs. Douglas's daughter and two grandchildren had lived with her a short time before they all moved away.

Coyle returned to the house and questioned all of the nearby neighbors he could find. Mrs. Connor, a widow who lived directly behind the Douglas place on the next street, was the only one who gave him a glimmer of hope.

"I reckon she didn't know where she was goin'. Leastways, if she did, she didn't confide in me," Mrs. Connor sniffed. "To tell you the gospel, I don't believe your wife ever cared much for me after I let it slip that Arminta was a-fixin' to marry that Mormon and become a convert to the LDS church."

Coyle nodded, thinking that it was typical of Emma to blame innocent people for things that irritated her. "But you have no idea where they went?" he persisted.

She shook her head. "I saw her load a trunk into a buggy, and she and the children drove out of town that way." She pointed west.

"Thanks. You've been a great help."

He took his leave, hardly knowing where to look next. He mounted his bay and gently neck-reined him down the street in a westerly direction, his distracted mind in a whirl. Somehow he had lost track of his wife and children. Only his first letter from Deadwood, four years ago, had been answered. In it, Emma had talked of routine things, avoiding any controversial topics. By the time he'd written back to her, she and the kids must have already moved, he thought, calculating the time. His next six letters, even after he'd gone on to Rapid City that November, had gone unanswered. He'd been hurt by that, but now realized that the mail had probably not reached her. But why hadn't she written to his last address at the hotel in Deadwood to say where she was going? Perhaps she had, but he and Crawford had been camped on the creeks for weeks. And, given the transient population in Deadwood, no one was going to make any Herculean efforts to deliver mail addressed to a man who had moved on.

He fought down the panic that surged up in his breast. He had lost them! He severely castigated himself for not returning to Denison immediately to look for them instead of just riding to Rapid City and going into the freighting business with Tom Merritt. Coyle rationalized that, four years ago, he couldn't have afforded the time or money for a trip to Iowa. As usual, he'd taken the easy course.

Maybe Emma had converted to Mormonism and gone with her mother and the new husband. Maybe Emma had divorced him on the grounds of desertion and married a Mormon herself to provide a home for her children. He'd heard that Mormons took care of their own, and that no one of their number ever suffered from poverty as long as the other members of the church had the means to prevent it. The possibility was almost too much for him to bear.

He pulled his horse to a stop in the middle of the deserted street, staring with unseeing eyes at the red orb sinking into a haze on the horizon. Emma and the kids were out there somewhere, and he meant to find them. But he had no idea how. He didn't even have the last name of Arminta's new husband. And the trail was already two years old.

Feeling the weight of guilt on his shoulders, he dismounted in front of a two-story white frame house. A sign suspended from the front porch roof read: ROOM AND BOARD — DAY, WEEK, OR MONTH. He was too weary and too despondent to camp out in some farmer's field that night.

Chapter Seven

December 22, 1881
Fort Meade, Dakota Territory

"By standing order, he's never to be ridden again," the corporal said, raising the earflaps of his fur cap in deference to the milder weather. "He has the run of the post. I'm assigned to keep him groomed and fed and his stall cleaned." He grinned boyishly. "The men let him drink beer out of a bucket. And he forages in the garbage cans outside the mess hall. I'm constantly having to clean spaghetti or beans off his face. Not too dignified for a symbol of the Seventh cavalry."

Thad Coyle smiled as he leaned against the white clapboard building that formed the end of a row of stables. Squinting against the glare of the sun off the snow, he studied the bay gelding, Comanche. The horse had gained national fame five years earlier as the only living thing found on the Custer battlefield. Coyle counted six scars showing through the rough winter coat — evidence of wounds that had spared him from being taken by the victorious Indians.

"Captain Keogh's horse," the corporal continued.

Coyle nodded, gazing at the sturdy animal that was cropping clumps of sparse grass between patches of melting snow. Maybe Comanche was not in the possession of the 7th cavalry because the regiment didn't want a living reminder of their worst disaster.

The gelding was about fifteen hands high, Coyle estimated, had a short sock on his left hind leg, extending halfway up the fetlock. There was also a small white star on his forehead. Coyle commented on the markings.

"Look at this," the corporal said, leading Coyle into the stables. He pointed at a printed verse posted prominently on the wall near a stall. Coyle read:

If you have a horse with four white feet,
   Keep him not a day;
If you have a horse with three white feet,
   Send him far away;
If you have a horse with two white feet,
   Sell him to a friend;
If you have a horse with one white foot,
   Keep him to the end.

"Sounds like some ancient horseman's adage."

"I don't know," the corporal shrugged. "Our company lieutenant found that poem in a book somewhere, and it just fit Comanche, since he has one white fetlock. And that star on his forehead is the luckiest of all."

Lucky for whom? Coyle wondered. Obviously Comanche had brought no luck to his owner, Captain Myles Keogh, or to the rest of Custer's command. But Coyle only replied: "Thanks for letting me see him."

"Any time." The corporal went back to his work while Coyle started along Officer's Row toward his waiting team and freight wagon.

Water was dripping from the roofs and gurgling down rain gutters as a bright sun and south wind softened the seven inches of snow. Coyle inhaled deeply, savoring the air that had lost its brittle edge in the brief December thaw.

It was three days until Christmas, and the gnawing void of loneliness was beginning to afflict him like it had at this season for the past five years. It happened as regularly as the sun retreating to its southern extremity. Each year he tried to numb himself to the emotional pain and endure it as best he could until the new year brought fresh hope and the promise of spring. He didn't try to analyze the reasons behind the melancholy, but it seemed to date from the year when he'd lost his family. Even Tom Merritt, his partner in the freighting business, noticed it and took pains to be especially considerate.

Coyle tried not to think about it as he looked at snow-capped Bear Butte, the sacred mountain of the Cheyennes, in the distance. It was a beautiful sight in the winter quiet. The entire post of Fort Meade seemed to be asleep, for that matter. This peacekeeper fort had been built here only three years earlier, and so far its troops had mostly participated in routine patrols. To date, this post near the Black Hills had become known for only one thing — the court-martial of Major Marcus Reno. After the death of his wife, the lonely Reno had become enamored of the daughter of the base commander. Reno had foolishly peered in the window of the commandant's house one evening after supper at the beautiful teenage girl who was reading a book by herself in the sitting room. Startled, she'd called out to her mother, and the commandant had Reno arrested. From what he'd read of the case, Coyle thought the whole thing had been blown out of proportion. One thing led to another, and Reno was tried for this incident and for getting drunk and fighting on post.

To Coyle, it appeared these minor indiscretions had been used to get Major Reno out of the Army. Since 1876, many within the military had sought to lay blame for the Custer massacre on Marcus Reno for his failure to come rapidly to the aid of Custer and his men during the fighting. The facts did not seem to support this accusation, but in the popular mind and press Reno was made to look like the scapegoat, nevertheless. Here was the perfect way to get rid of the embarrassing Reno. And get rid of him they did. In spite of several high-ranking dissenting voices, Reno was convicted of conduct unbecoming an officer and discharged from the service. Unlike most others who followed the case in the papers, Coyle could relate to what Reno was going through. Not only relate, but he could feel the major's pain like a knife in his own gut. Reading about the court-martial brought back the anguish of five years earlier.

Which house was it? he wondered, as he walked past the big, two-story homes. One of these houses was the commandant's where Reno had been caught as a peeping Tom. He shook his head and looked away. He was already feeling depressed enough, in spite of the sunny, mid-winter thaw. No sense dredging up the past to torment himself further. He would climb on his wagon and get back to

Sturgis where Tom Merritt was waiting. They'd have an early supper and maybe a little wine. But he had to be careful about the drinking. He didn't want alcohol to become an escape from his moods.

He came in sight of his team of mules, steaming in the sunshine. One was tossing his head to get the last of the grain out of his feedbag. The number of brass-bound kegs of beer and wooden cases of wine and other spirits the enlisted commissary men had just unloaded from his wagon would be enough to keep every man and woman on this post drunk for more than a week. Coyle wondered what was done with such a supply. Some of the expensive spirits would probably disappear into the liquor cabinets of the higher ranking officers. Coyle reflected that duty on this post would be very boring. In such an atmosphere, he knew that mounted drill, inspections, and military minutiæ took on exaggerated importance, since soldiers in a peacetime atmosphere had nothing else to do. There would be much gambling and drinking and fighting. But desertions would be down this time of year, as the snowbirds needed a place to eat and sleep, more than they needed the thirteen dollars a month a private earned.

Just ahead of him a figure in a hooded cloak came out from between two large houses. It was a woman carrying a basket on her arm, and she turned toward him along the wide street. She was hurrying, apparently preoccupied and looking down. Her face, from this distance, was pretty, framed by dark hair and the hood. He looked closer. There was something about the way she moved, the nose, the shape of her face.

He stopped, stunned. "Emma!"

She jerked her head up, startled. Their eyes locked. Coyle could feel his heart suddenly thumping wildly. Yet he felt paralyzed. He couldn't move or speak. A rush of emotion flooded him. He swallowed twice.

"Thad. . . ."

They approached each other tentatively. How would she react? Had she wanted to get rid of him? What should he say?

She dropped her basket and sprang forward. He enveloped her in his arms.

"God, Emma," he whispered hoarsely, his face in her hair. "I thought I'd lost you forever."

Then he was kissing her, feeling her chilled lips and skin.

After several long seconds, she pulled back, breathless. He held her at arm's length. She was even more beautiful than he remembered, her cheeks flushed with cold and excitement, her white, even teeth smiling, lively eyes drinking him in.

"What . . . what are you doing here?" he managed to gasp.

"I was delivering some fancy cakes for an officers' party. I run a small bakery out of my place in town. What about you?"

"I'm in partnership in a freighting business. I just dropped off several cases of liquid refreshment and some other things. But never mind that now. I don't know how we lost track of each other, but we've got a lot of catching up to do."

"Yes. Yes." She slid into his arms again.

When they separated, he picked up the wicker basket she had dropped.

"My buggy is down near the end of the parade ground," she said.

"I'll walk with you. My wagon's back the other way. I want to hear all about the kids. And there is a lot I want to say to you."

She slipped off her leather gloves, and he held her cold fingers as they walked slowly along in the warming sunshine.

After they finally found each other, he and Emma stayed together for three years. He dissolved his partnership with Tom Merritt and moved to Washington, D.C., where he was able to land a job as a clerk with the Indian Bureau. The pay was barely adequate, but the work was steady, and he was home every night with his wife and two children, whom he'd missed even more than he realized. He began again to watch his son and daughter grow. Now, at ages ten and twelve, they had both been attending school for several years.

But, then, good times, as well as bad, never seemed to last. Change was the only constant. Emma got pregnant. At first elated and radiant, her demeanor gradually changed as the weeks wore on. When their son was born, his blue lips and fingernails were an outward indication of a congenital heart defect. The baby, whom they christened David, lived only three months. The doctors said there was nothing that could be done for him, so Coyle had already resigned himself to this fact when they found the infant dead in his crib one morning.

The clods of dirt thumping on the tiny coffin that cold March day signaled more than anguish for them. Emma, suffering not only from grief but from depression, had blamed Coyle for the tragedy. Her reaction was a complete mystery to him. There was no plausible explanation for her bitter reproaches. He could do nothing to please her. It was as if she were transferring all her unhappiness to him. The constant rebuffs and heavy silences hurt like a ball of ice in his stomach. After two weeks, he finally stopped trying and left her alone with her pain.

Returning from work late one afternoon, he got off the trolley, walked up the street to their rented house, and found that she'd left and taken the two children. A note left on the kitchen table was brief; she couldn't stand to live with him any more. No word of where she had gone, and if or when she might return. As dusk came on, he sat in the front parlor of the silent house, oil lamp turned low on the table beside his chair. For one of the few times in his life, he wept bitter tears. After a time, he was able to calm himself long enough to realize that her leaving was due to nothing he had done. The irrational response had to be the result of some imbalance, something that caused the compulsive behavior beyond her ability to control it. It was not a thought-out hatred of him. It was merely nature's reaction to the trauma her body and mind had suffered from the birth and death of the baby.

He sat, staring through the window at the dark street outside, sipping a glass of Chianti. At midnight he went to bed. Sleep would temporarily blot out the hurt.

When, after a month, he had no word of Emma, Coyle actively sought assignments outside of his Washington office. In his three years with the Indian Bureau, he'd risen to a position of adviser to newly appointed Indian agents. Without revealing his court-martial, he called on his experience with various Indian tribes to brief some of the spoils system appointees on what to expect. He was promoted to the position of Special Indian Agent, a job that was still low enough to be protected by the recently enacted Civil Service Act. He wangled a temporary assignment to check on conditions at San Carlos in the Arizona Territory where several Apache bands were unhappily confined. He had assisted the agent in charge with pertinent suggestions for improving conditions on the reservation. He reported that unless Indian policy changed, or the Apaches were relocated, there would be no short-term solution. His message was not welcome, but his diplomacy and insight later got him sent to other reservations in the West. He had a personal knack of giving advice without giving offense. Since his court-martial, he'd learned to bend and not to confront belligerently.

His travel and his job became distractions from the second loss of his family. As the months passed, he could only hope that Emma would come to her senses and contact him. He remained in the small rented house just outside Washington so she would be able to write to him. Yet no word came. The pain dulled, but it never went away.

Chapter Eight

August 24, 1890
Badlands of South Dakota

The Oglala ghost dance camp was deathly quiet.

United States Special Indian Agent Thad Coyle let his gaze drift over the more than twelve dozen white canvas lodges pitched among the cabins of Torn Belly's permanent camp. Not a sign of life. Hot prairie wind spiraled smoke away from a hundred abandoned cooking fires. An American flag flapped atop a pole in a wide circle of bare earth.

"Maybe they're all observing the Sabbath," Coyle commented dryly to Hugh Gallagher, the Pine Ridge agent who rode beside him.

"Huh! They've got religion, all right," Gallagher muttered, "but this damned ghost dance religion is a perversion of all the Christian teachings they've been exposed to." He frowned.

Coyle felt his sarcasm miss its mark, and let it drop. Gallagher, a former Union officer, was a humorless man who took everything literally. Probably just as well the old man was being put out to pasture by the spoils system. Being an Indian agent on a reservation was not a job for a man with no imagination, a man who went strictly by the book and by policy. An agent had to be able to bend with the wind and improvise when circumstances demanded. The new Republican Administration had already notified Gallagher he was to be replaced. That was the reason Coyle had been sent here a week ago — to smooth the change over.

The two white men, along with half-blood interpreter Phillip Wells, rode at the head of twenty uniformed Lakota tribal police — "metal breasts" their fellow Sioux called them, referring to the large metal badges they wore. Coyle reflected that without the loyalty of young Sioux men who volunteered to join the tribal police, the civilian agents probably could not keep order among the unruly element on the six remaining Sioux reservations in the Dakotas.

Last Friday, Gallagher had ordered a party of tribal police to inform Torn Belly no more ghost dancing would be permitted. Coyle had been in the agent's office yesterday when the police lieutenant reported back, stating the ghost dancers had subjected them to the vilest insults and driven them off at gunpoint.

110

"By God, they've got gall!" Gallagher had exploded, slamming his fist on his desk. "I'll ride out there tomorrow and see what's going on. Are you up for it, Coyle?"

The police detail was put on notice, and they'd started at half past seven this morning, the sun already hot on their backs and the incessant prairie wind blowing from the south. Three hours of trotting and walking their mounts had brought them to the banks of White Clay Creek on the edge of the Badlands. The creek wound through a picturesque grassy valley near buff-colored, eroded buttes and mesas. An irregular fringe of cottonwoods marked the watercourse, their dusty green leaves stirring in the breeze, while unseen roots probed deep for moisture.

The horses' hoofs scuffed puffs of dust from beneath the parched grass as the riders drew rein on the edge of the bare dance ground. Two warriors sprang suddenly from the cover of the cottonwoods, each dropping to one knee and leveling his Winchester.

"We come to parlay with Torn Belly," Coyle said quickly, his heart beginning to pound at the sight of those unwavering black muzzles.

But Gallagher reacted in character, kneeing his horse forward. "What do you mean, drawing your guns on me when I come to you as your father agent?" he demanded, his face reddening.

Coyle cringed at the adversarial tone, sensing trouble. But interpreter Wells, spurred his horse forward in front of the agent, speaking quickly in the guttural Sioux language. He gestured to the two warriors as several more armed Indians darted from the cabins toward the cover of the creekbank. Wells appeared to address one of them by name.

"What're you saying?" Gallagher demanded.

"I told them you come in peace and asked them to lower their guns so we could talk," Wells replied smoothly.

The warrior addressed lowered his rifle and placed it on the ground.

A real diplomat, Coyle thought, exhaling. But then one of the other warriors called out in English: "If you have come to talk to us as our father agent, why do you bring so many guns?"

Other armed Sioux appeared, and one of them shouted: "Where is Thunder Bear? Are you afraid to show your face? Hanging back like a woman?"

The police lieutenant thus addressed urged his horse forward. "Here I am! If you cannot see far, I will ride closer to you!"

The other tribal police began drawing their pistols, and Coyle heard the metallic *chunking* of repeating rifles being cocked from the cover of the creekbank and the trees. He slipped his toes from his stirrups and looked for a spot to dive on the ground if lead started flying.

Just then a tall, straight Indian galloped between the two clashing forces and held up his hand, holding his prancing mount on a tight rein. In the few seconds of silence that followed, Coyle heard Wells mutter the name: "Young-Man-Afraid-Of-His-Horses." Apparently this son of an influential chief of the Oglalas carried much authority, and the tension began to melt. Coyle's hand relaxed, and his Remington slid back into its holster. In the space of two long breaths, the charged atmosphere was broken as the Sioux lowered their rifles and began appearing in the open.

Five minutes later, the two groups were mingling on the bare dance ground near the flagpole. Coyle hung back and observed as Gallagher and Phillip Wells parlayed with Torn Belly and the other leaders whom Wells later would identify as Bear Bone, His Fight, and Jack Red Cloud, son of the famous chief.

They all sat cross-legged on the ground, facing each other. Coyle watched and listened, sensing that Wells was couching in more diplomatic language the agent's demands that the ghost dance stop. The exchange was friendly enough, but it was soon evident that Torn Belly and the other three leaders were adamantly refusing to stop what they considered their right to practice their new religious ceremony of the dance.

As blunt as he was, Gallagher apparently thought discretion was the better part of valor — especially in the camp of a very agitated enemy. To Coyle's relief, Gallagher showed the good sense to acquiesce and even asked if their party could stay and observe the dance.

The expressionless Torn Belly almost smiled. He rose and said something in Lakota. The crowd of men and women began to move toward what looked to be a parade ground.

"He says for you to be seated and watch while the dance begins," Wells translated to the two agents.

Coyle positioned himself on one side of Wells as the three of them, along with the twenty tribal police, dispersed along the windward side of the dance ground. Coyle was glad for the opportunity to find out, firsthand, what this ghost dance business was all about.

Wells was much more white than Indian in physical appearance, with light skin and a heavy mustache. This, added to his clothing and educated speech, made him nearly indistinguishable from a full-blood white. But he had an insight into Lakota thinking that Coyle meant to tap.

More than two hundred Indians formed two concentric circles while Torn Belly stood in the middle with Bear Bone near the flagpole, apparently giving instructions in Lakota.

"Well?" Coyle looked curiously at Wells who was listening closely.

"He's telling them that they are ready for the dance because they have purified themselves in the sweat lodges."

"Before we got here?"

Wells nodded.

The dancers then broke up into small groups, and the leaders and their assistants decorated the faces. Forehead, cheeks, and chins were painted with circles, crescents, and crosses that symbolized the sun, moon, and morning star, Wells explained quietly. Red represented the color of the sun. The dancers were fully clothed, many of them in buckskin leggings and ghost shirts of cotton, or doeskin, decorated with symbols of eagles, magpies, deer, sage hens, and the planets — all significant in Sioux mythology. Wells pointed out that most of the dancers wore eagle feathers in their hair. "Helps them ascend to the spirit world," he explained. "And that's not just a flagpole in the middle," he added. "It's a prayer tree. Sometimes they cut a big pine and stand it up, then put decorations on it . . . presents to the gods and all kinds of stuff."

"Almost like a Christmas tree," Gallagher said. "My police tell me these dancers believe the Messiah is coming again to the Indians."

"Bringing their dead ancestors and friends and plenty of buffalo," Wells said. "Supposedly the earth is worn out and will be covered with a new layer of dirt that will bury all the whites."

"Convenient," Gallagher grunted.

"You're half-white and half-Lakota," Coyle said. "Where does that leave you?"

Wells shrugged. "I don't think their theology touches on that point."

"When is this supposed to happen?"

"Sometime in the spring."

The people of both sexes and all ages sat on the ground in two concentric circles, facing inward. Torn Belly was flanked by his assistants, Jack Red Cloud, Bear Bone, and His Fight. Jack Red Cloud raised his arms, closed his eyes, and prayed in English, apparently for the benefit of the agents: "Great Waken Takan, we are ready to begin the dance as you have commanded us. Our hearts are good. We beg you to give us back our hunting grounds and the buffalo." Heavy black hair framed the smooth, bronze face and strong

116

nose of the young leader.

Coyle wondered if races who did not grow facial hair tended to wear their hair long to compensate.

"Take those who are most worthy to the Spirit Land and let them see their dead relatives and all the wonderful things you have prepared for us. Then return them safely to earth. We beg you to hear our prayer."

The people in the circles stood and joined hands. Then Torn Belly and Jack Red Cloud started a rhythmic chant.

> Someone come to tell the news, to tell
>   the news,
> There will be a buffalo chase.
> Make arrows, make arrows.

The people joined the singing, a few at a time until the whole circle began to feel the rhythm. Knees bent in time to the ghost song, their bodies rising and falling. Then the circle began a slow, shuffle step to the left as they chanted the non-melodic rhythm.

> The whole world is coming,
> A nation is coming, a nation is coming,
> The eagle has brought the message to
>   the tribe.
> The Father says so, the Father says so.

117

The volume rose, and the tempo quickened. Some of the lead singers lapsed into the Lakota language, and the dancers followed.

So far the whole thing was pretty tame. *Nothing to get alarmed about.* He moved back a few feet to get a better view of the dance and to avoid the dust that was being churned up by the shuffling of the moccasined feet on the outer edges of the hard-packed ground.

After about thirty minutes, the dance was stopped, and the dance leader cried: "Weep for your sins!"

A great moaning welled up from the crowd, pierced by the high-pitched wails of individuals. Some dancers rolled on the ground, crying out for forgiveness while others cut their arms with bone knives in the ancient way of showing grief. Some of the blood flowing down their arms they smeared on the prayer tree, while others took off trinkets and feathers from their clothing and tied them as gifts to the prayer tree.

Still not much different from the more extreme white Fundamentalists.

At a signal from Torn Belly, the dancers seated themselves, and the leader exhorted them in their own language.

"A sermon," Wells said quietly. "Reminding them to do as the Messiah has commanded them and they will soon be free of all white men, and everything will be restored and renewed." Wells paused. "You notice that nothing is carried that is of white manufacture? Even the knives are of stone or bone. The cloth shirts and some of the beads on the moccasins are the only exceptions . . . but only because they have no hides to make clothing. The same with the canvas teepees."

At the leader's word, the dancers stood and resumed the shuffling, left-moving circle. But now they moved faster, showing more emotion, chanting of the future.

> The people are coming home,
> The people are coming home
> Says my father, says my father.
> The time comes, I will see him,
> The time comes, I will see him
> Says my mother, says my mother.

Faster and faster the circles moved, the dancers bending and weaving. Coyle had to look away every few seconds to keep from getting dizzy at the constant stream of undulating motion just in front of his eyes. It was like watching a fast merry-go-round. Some of the dancers shrieked and leaped into the air. The chanting broke up into wails and shouting as the people worked themselves into a frenzy.

The leaders dashed around the inside of the

circles, exhorting the dancers to even greater excitement. Here and there a man or woman fell or was eased to the ground by the leaders, in an apparent swoon.

"They're being transported to the spirit world," Wells said, staring intently at the spectacle.

The fire in the interpreter's eyes seemed to reflect the aboriginal side of his nature — a longing for the bliss and vision of the spirit world he'd been taught was inaccessible in this life.

Some, who did not achieve their goal of being caught up into another dimension, rushed blindly out of the circle, butting their heads against the startled horses and falling to the ground. Two crashed into the prayer tree.

After another two hours, the remaining dancers were so exhausted they could barely stagger, while many rolled on the ground, screaming and moaning.

The sun was halfway down the western sky, but the late August heat was still oppressive. Coyle credited the ever-constant wind for preserving some of the people from heat stroke. Dust stuck to the sweaty, painted faces that were contorted in agonies of effort. Every dancer strained to be snatched up temporarily from earth-bound existence.

The Indian police hunkered in the shade of

the cottonwoods in small groups, smoking cigarettes and impassively watching the ceremony. Their black eyes revealed nothing of their feelings as they spoke quietly to one another.

A man and woman collapsed almost simultaneously, the man frothing at the mouth, wild eyes seeing something beyond. A chill went up Coyle's sweaty back.

Dozens, who had fallen exhausted, struggled to their feet after a time and danced on until late afternoon when the leaders called a halt for supper. The dancers and leaders alike seemed to have forgotten the presence of their visitors.

As they squatted around the cooking fires, one of the dancers was waving his arms and proclaiming that he'd been transported to the spirit world.

"I have seen visions of the Messiah who showed me wonderful things!" he cried to all within earshot. A crowd began to gravitate toward him.

"He's seen visions, sure enough," snorted Hugh Gallagher under his breath, "but they were all inside his head."

"I wept when I looked at His beautiful face," the visionary continued, "because He had nail marks in His hands, and, when He moved, the feather mantle He wore shifted and I could see the lance wound in His side. He came to the whites long ago, and they nailed Him to a cross!" Emotion twisted the dark face as he shouted. Sweat streaked the red and yellow paint. "The Messiah insisted we continue the dance and promised that no whites would enter His land or have any of the good things He has promised to the Indians!"

"I was also taken to the world of the spirits!" a woman shouted. "When I fell into a trance, the Messiah showed me my dead children, my friends, and the old people who are gone from the earth. They were all healthy and young and rode beautiful horses." Several dozen dancers pushed closer to hear her, some still eating. "I was carried away by an eagle with great wings." She spread her arms to indicate the giant raptor. "I was taken over a hill, and there was a village such as we had before whites came into our country. The teepees were made of buffalo hide, and the People were using the bow and arrow. There was nothing made by whites. The land was green, with flowing streams, and filled with herds of buffalo, elk, and deer. The Messiah told me the earth was now bad and worn out, and we needed a new dwelling place where the bad whites could not disturb us. He told me to return to my people and continue the dance. We should pay no attention to the whites. If the high priests make medicine shirts and pray over them, no harm can come to the dancers who wear them. If any whites shoot at them, the bullets will drop without harm. The shooters will fall down dead into a hole in the earth where the Messiah has prepared hot water and fire for them."

Even though women in Indian society did all the work, except for hunting, and were servants to their men, they seemed to have an equal status when it came to this new religion. Their voices were listened to, Coyle noted. He chewed a piece of gritty, fried bread as he absorbed this extraordinary tale. Other tribes in years past had preached immunity from white bullets, along with a mish-mash of their own myths and Christian teachings. But the Sioux were the only ones perverting this current religious craze to include bulletproof ghost shirts.

He looked around for something else to eat, but saw nothing he wanted to try. He passed up the simmering pots of stew into which the Indians dipped their cups and bowls. It was a fortnight since the last beef issue, and Coyle was suspicious of the unusual absence of dogs in the camp.

When everyone had finished eating, the dancing resumed, gradually building to a crescendo as before. Several larger fires were

kindled for illumination as the sun dropped
below the buttes of the Badlands and the long
summer twilight came on.

> I've given you my strength,
> Says the father, says the father.
> The shirt will cause you to live,
> Says the father, says the father.

Coyle was growing weary of the monoto-
nous chanting and shuffling. But as darkness
closed down, the screams of the frenzied began to take on an ominous quality. Before he
realized how much time had passed, Gallagher was touching his shoulder.

"Time to go."

Coyle got stiffly to his feet. He saw the
tribal police preparing to mount up.

"I've seen all I need to see," Gallagher said,
brushing off his clothes.

"This will go on till at least midnight,"
Wells said, throwing a saddle onto his horse.
"Or until nobody can stand any more."

Coyle took a last look at the eerily gyrating
figures back-lighted by the blazing cottonwood limbs. The hysteria seemed to be reaching a peak. He mounted and pulled his
horse's head around, following Phillip Wells
and Hugh Gallagher out into the darkness, as
the Lakota police strung out behind. The

party began its twenty-mile ride back to the agency.

There was no conversation as they rode in the moonless darkness over the gently rolling grassland. Away from the smoke and dust, the stars were sharp points of light in the clear vault of sky.

Yet the images of the frenzied dancers gyrating wildly against the firelight was burned into Coyle's retina. The rhythm of the chanting still throbbed in his ears, even after they were long out of hearing. The ghost dancers were wild with self-induced delirium. But, at least, they apparently didn't use hallucinatory drugs, as did the peyote cult of the Comanches.

As strange as the ghost dance appeared, Coyle felt no threat from what he'd just seen and heard. Contrary to the pacifist teachings of Wovoka, Winchesters had appeared in the hands of some Sioux dancers. If the Messiah were really going to eliminate the white race when He returned, the more militant Lakotas appeared willing to give Him some human help. But still, there seemed no real reason for alarm just yet. True, the white settlers near the reservation were crying wolf and loudly demanding that Gallagher put a stop to the ghost dance before it turned violent. They were all predicting a bloody uprising.

Coyle sighed. If the political wheels ground at their usual ponderous pace, he would probably inherit this mess for weeks, or even months, before the new agent was appointed. Would he have authority to proceed as he saw fit, or would every decision have to be cleared through Washington by telegram? One wrong move and he could be unemployed just as Gallagher was about to be.

He glanced at the vast, starry firmament. How peaceful those far-off stars appeared — each in its place in some sort of complex pattern, unlike the affairs of men. He often speculated on the reasons for things and how situations evolved. He pondered the series of decisions that had led him, at age forty-seven, to be sitting on the edge of a potential Sioux uprising. He'd always assumed that, when he reached middle age, the grief and hardships that came to men in their prime would be left behind. His intellect and experience told him the ghost dance would die out of its own accord with the coming of the harsh Dakota winter. But a tiny, persistent flame of uneasiness in his stomach alerted him that he could be wrong. By what circuitous route had he ridden into this box cañon?

Chapter Nine

November 12, 1890
Pine Ridge Agency, South Dakota

The single, wide street of the Pine Ridge Agency was swarming with Indians as Coyle stepped off the shaded porch of the agency offices. Canvas-topped wagons were parked everywhere. Sioux families in their best clothing thronged the three trading posts and milled in the street, visiting. It was close to noon, and they had been arriving all morning from the far reaches of the reservation.

Coyle leaned against a porch post and watched the gathering, reflecting that in the circumscribed lives of these reservation people the semi-monthly beef and ration issue day had taken on great importance as an opportunity to socialize. And today the weather was also co-operating, the temperature approaching sixty with some high, thin clouds.

Indian police were stationed at strategic points, guarding the agency offices, keeping a close watch on the traders' posts and the commissary, as well as the corral with a small beef herd. As he turned to look at the dark, impassive face of the policeman on the porch behind him, Coyle wondered what the man was thinking. A uniform, a badge, and a few dollars a month did not convert an aborigine into a white man. For the most part these police were men in their twenties who had never known the old ways of tribal life, the days of following buffalo herds, bowing to the wisdom of the elder chiefs and the medicine men, proving their manhood by raiding enemies, counting coup, and stealing horses — horses later used to barter for a bride. Maybe it was better these young Sioux did not remember those days when whites were the enemy of the People and there were no divided loyalties. To them, being a policeman for the whites was now the only way to earn some money and to prove their manhood.

Coyle pushed the hat up from his forehead, wishing he hadn't worn the leather vest that was rapidly becoming too warm in the sun. But he quickly forgot his discomfort as he saw Molly Seeker, one of the agency schoolteachers, threading her way through the crowd toward him. She carried no parasol and wore no bonnet or hat to shield her fair skin from the sun. She wore a short jacket over a white blouse, and her pointed boots peeked out from under the long skirt as she walked. He'd met Molly in late September at a dinner given by the wife of one of the post traders and had been immediately struck by her confident practicality. A spinster in her early thirties, she was not beautiful, but did have a pleasant face and what he guessed was a well-rounded figure. He had taken to calling on her whenever he got a chance, but hadn't seen her for more than a week. Her teaching at the boarding school took up all her time and energy. But school had been dismissed for ration day.

"Hello, Molly," he said as she approached. "Going down to watch the beef issue?"

"I've seen it before." She shrugged. "But there's not much else to do."

They joined the crowd gravitating toward the corral on the south side of town. Even before they got close, herders swung open the gate and released three steers. Whooping and yelling, several Sioux men galloped toward the panicked cattle. Carbines cracked somewhere in the swirling dust, and the steers went down in a pale imitation of the old ways of hunting buffalo.

Maneuvering for an unobstructed view, Coyle saw several more steers released in quick succession. The animals ran only a few yards before they were headed off, then stumbled, and fell under the rifle fire.

"Didn't the Indian Bureau recently outlaw this shooting of cattle?" she asked. "Calling it a barbarous custom?" A few strands of blonde hair escaped the tight bun at the back of her head as she squinted at him in the wan November sunshine.

He nodded. "You're right. Maybe my bosses think that hitting them in the head in the Omaha and Chicago slaughterhouses is somehow more humane."

She shook her head and turned back to watch the spectacle, one hand shading her eyes.

The beef issue had been cut, and the shooting excitement was soon over. Dust and gunsmoke drifted away as the rest of the Indians descended on the fresh carcasses with knives to skin and dress the meat. It would then be divided among the families present.

Coyle accompanied Molly back up the street, talking. As they passed the commissary, a group of brightly dressed Sioux women were lining up with cloth sacks to draw their small allotment of flour, bacon, coffee, and sugar. Farther along, other Indians were crowding into the three traders' posts to buy and barter for goods. Coyle glanced in the window of the dispensary as they passed. Dr. Charles Eastman, a fullblood Santee Sioux, had returned to the reservation to treat his own people and was examining an Indian patient. The dispensary shared a building with the police assembly room. Coyle knew the leaders of the Oglalas had taken advantage of this gathering to meet in council inside the assembly room.

Just as he and Molly passed this one-story wooden structure, Lt. Thunder Bear and a squad of six uniformed tribal policemen swept past them, and suddenly Coyle heard voices shouting a few yards away. He turned to see the police taking the arms of Little, a young Sioux man who was dressed in white man's pants and blue and white polka-dotted shirt.

"You're under arrest for killing agency cattle. The agent wants to see you!" the voice of Thunder Bear cut through the din.

With a move like a coiling rattlesnake, Little jerked loosed and sprang back against the wall of the building. A long butcher knife appeared in his hand.

Coyle grabbed Molly's arm and dragged her quickly away as a wave of ghost dancers surged up around Little, shouting and brandishing knives and rifles. The squad of police was quickly surrounded.

"Kill the metal breasts!"

"Burn the agency!"

"We have the power!"

Shouts came in English from a dozen throats, dark faces aflame with bitterness and hate.

Coyle looked quickly for a safe place of retreat. They were still a good distance from the agency offices. With one arm around Molly, he loosened the big Remington pistol in its holster.

"Stop! Think!" A deep voice cut through the yelling, and the crowd noise rumbled down to silence within a few seconds.

They stepped up onto a porch across the street, and Coyle looked back to see the imposing figure of American Horse, a battle-hardened old chief who was moving out of the council room. He wore striped pants and a black coat. His broad nose and wide mouth were clearly visible above the heads of the crowd as he stood on the bottom step of the porch.

"What are you going to do?" American Horse thundered at them. "Kill these men of our own race? Then what? Kill all these helpless white men and women? And what then? What will these brave words, brave deeds, lead to in the end? How long can you hold out? Your country is surrounded with a network of railroads. Thousands of white soldiers will be here within three days. Do you have enough ammunition? What provisions?

What will become of your families? Think, think, my brothers! This is a child's madness."

There followed an uneasy silence as the power and persuasion of this respected elder seemed to dampen their blood lust. Everyone there knew that American Horse was no coward. He had been one of the chiefs who had fought General Crook and others in the old days, when there was still a chance of winning.

Coyle held his breath. Just when he thought the crisis had passed, Jack Red Cloud, one of the leaders of the ghost dance at Torn Belly's camp, pushed through the mob and shoved a cocked revolver at the speaker, the muzzle only inches from his face.

"It's you and your kind who've brought us to this!"

Even from across the street, Coyle could make out the look of utter disdain on the old chief's face. Without another word, American Horse turned away and slowly mounted the steps to the council room and closed the door behind him. The helpless police squad watched the mob disperse.

Three days later Coyle sat in an empty office of the Pine Ridge Agency and looked around at the desks, the chairs, the pine floor — everything was coated with a fine layer of

Dakota topsoil. He'd been sneezing on and off most of the morning, and his head felt as if it were packed with wet sawdust. He thrust a large bandanna back into his hip pocket and tried vainly to force air through his swollen nasal passages. Breathing through his mouth had made it dry and gritty from the blowing dust. To him, the powdery irritant was merely an exasperating inconvenience. He wondered idly if inhaling this several months a year might account for the prevalence of consumption among the native Sioux who lived close to the soil on this reservation. That, plus improper diet and unsanitary living conditions. Normally frost or rain would have put a literal damper on the dust by mid-November, but this year had been different. The weather had not co-operated. A dry summer had been followed by a dry autumn. Winter had taken a couple of tentative steps toward them with a light dusting of snow on November 6th. Then, two days later, the first blizzard gusted down from the north, with swirling snow and temperatures in the low teens. But November 10th had dawned bright and clear, and a warm sun and south wind quickly melted the four inches of snow so that, two days later, there was no indication of winter's first blast. The weather had reverted to mild days and cool nights.

And the ghost dancing had continued, even increased in intensity among its adherents. Yet, even though more than half of all the Sioux on Pine Ridge and the other reservations had nothing to do with the new religion, the new agent was in a panic, fearing an imminent uprising.

Daniel J. Royer had been the spoils system appointee who replaced Hugh Gallagher the first week of October. Royer, a pharmacist, physician, and banker from Alpena, South Dakota, had no previous experience with Indians of any kind. Two terms in the territorial legislature was his sole qualification for the job. Outwardly there was nothing distinctive about Royer. He was a short man in his forties who wore a drooping mustache and habitually overdressed in starched shirt, heavily knotted tie, vest, watch chain, topcoat, and gray bowler. More important, he was of an extremely nervous disposition. Lacking any personal forcefulness or administrative skills, he had been crying wolf ever since the first week he had taken office at Pine Ridge. The ghost dancing had immediately alarmed him. Under written orders to stop the dancing, Royer had passed the order to the Indians who quickly sensed the fear emanating from the man and ignored him. Frustrated and fearful, Royer had not known what to do but go on repeating the order from the safety of his office every few days. At the same time he busied himself sending urgent letters and telegrams to Washington, predicting dire consequences if immediate help was not forthcoming in the form of troops to quell the barbarians under his care. Sensing that Royer was not up to the task, Coyle's bosses at the Interior Department had told him to stay on for an indefinite period in an advisory capacity until the situation settled down.

Coyle leaned back in his chair, draped one leg across a corner of the desk, and laced his fingers behind his head. For now, at least, he didn't have to listen to Agent Royer's constant, fearful whining and dire predictions. Royer, leaving word that his nerves needed a little rest, had taken a buggy yesterday afternoon and driven twenty-five miles south, off the reservation, to the railroad town of Rushville, Nebraska, where he planned to spend a few days at the hotel.

In spite of Coyle's calming assurances that the ghost dance phenomenon would subside with time when the Messiah didn't appear, Royer had taken to pacing around the office, reading aloud his latest missive to the Commissioner of Indian Affairs, and waving his hands, pausing only long enough to ask: "That's right, isn't it? You agree with that,

136

don't you? Isn't that the way you see it?"

As if protecting himself from future reper-
cussions, Royer had employed Molly Seeker
to make typewritten copies of all correspondence for the agency records. Coyle opened a
file drawer and took out copies of the two
most recent letters to the commissioner. The
first had been written on ration day just after
the abortive attempt to arrest the defiant Indian, Little. Coyle scanned the letter. It read,
in part:

Today I ordered . . . the police force to
arrest an Indian that had violated the
law in several instances, one of the
charges being that he has been killing
cattle promiscuously on the reservation.
He drew his knife and positively refused
to be arrested, and a mob of the ghost
dancers rushed in and relieved thei'
fellow dancer from the hands of t'
police, taking him away to their car
and boasting of their power and m'
all kinds of fun over the attempter'
and the inefficiency of the
force. . . .

The second letter had beer
day, just before Royer's dep
his eyes down the sheet.

137

Your Department has been informed of the damage resulting from these dances and of the danger attending them of the crazy Indians doing serious damage to others, and the different Agencies, I suppose, report about the same, but I have carefully studied the matter for nearly six weeks and have brought all the persuasion to bear on the leaders that was possible but without effect, and the only remedy for this matter is the use of military force, and until this is done you need not expect any progress from these people, on the other hand you will be made to realize that they are tearing down more in a day than the government can build in a month.

I hope the commissioner took a deep breath before he tried to read that *heavy sentence aloud,* Coyle thought with a smile. Royer was a man out of place if there ever was one. In fact, the Oglalas, during the first week had dubbed im "Young-Man-Afraid-Of-Indians." Coyle got up and walked to a side window ere he could view most of the frame build- at Pine Ridge Agency. No protective dbreak of trees had been planted around gency buildings. They stood naked to the nts, the sun and winds weathering and

warping the one-time whitewashed boards, shrinking doors until they didn't fit, allowing dust or snow to sift in through the cracks. Yet this was luxury compared to the way most of the Indians lived. Even those who had abandoned their teepees for permanent dwellings of cottonwood logs usually made do with only packed earth for floors and a piece of canvas or hide for a door.

A wide, dirt street separated the two scattered groups of agency buildings. At the end of the street was the only multi-storied building — the agency boarding school that could hold about two hundred students. At present a hundred sixty-six children were being housed and taught there. He picked out the supply storehouse, the employees' quarters, the ice and meat house, and the drab police barracks. On the far side of several small structures, about a quarter mile away, was the steeple of the Episcopal church. The Episcopalians, along with the Catholics, Congregationalists, and Presbyterians, had made quite a number of converts among the various Sioux tribes spread across the six reservations in North and South Dakota.

Several children ran down the street, romping with two dogs. Two Sioux women, blankets around their shoulders, walked together nearby. There was no sign of any of the blue uniforms of the tribal police. A deceptively quiet day.

Having been an Army officer, as well as an employee of the Interior Department, Coyle was very aware of the long rivalry between military and civilians for control of reservation Indians. Army officers had for years been scornful of the pacification program advocated by succeeding Commissioners of Indian Affairs. In an effort to secure agents who were both honest and conscientious, the Interior Department had actively recruited and appointed members of the Society of Friends — Quakers — as Indian agents.

As far as Coyle knew, Royer was not a Quaker, but his continuing calls for military help were very likely influencing new President Benjamin Harrison in the direction of placing the military in charge of the reservations. In Coyle's mind, it was only a matter of time before this happened. General Nelson Miles, commander of the Department of the Missouri, had long advocated military control.

He sighed and turned away from the window. Another major problem was the warmongering of the bigger newspapers in the East. A dozen or more reporters had been sent here to cover the ghost dance frenzy and resulting tensions. As much as he hated to see it, these competing reporters had to placate their bosses and justify their own expenses by manufacturing a non-existent war. SETTLERS ALARMED, REPORTS OF KILLINGS AND RANCH BURNINGS, TENSIONS RUNNING HIGH, SIOUX ARMING FOR UPRISING, OUTBREAK IMMINENT — all the tricks of innuendo and rumor were reported as news stories. Taking all this at face value, the average reader would conclude a bloody Indian war was due to break out at any moment. Some of the headlines Coyle had seen were so ludicrous that any reasonable person would have laughed at them. But, he thought, most readers had never seen a Sioux Indian and knew nothing of the situation except what they read in their local papers. And that episode three days ago would do nothing to quiet the situation.

Coyle felt he could deal calmly and impartially with events as they unfolded, except for one thing — a reporter for the *Omaha Bee* who had arrived ten days ago was none other than Thomas Carson, formerly a corporal in the 23rd infantry at Fort Hartsuff. The thought of this man from his past brought such a stab of pain that Coyle had taken to having at least two drinks at the trader's store after supper each night to relax himself enough to sleep. He had seen the former soldier from a distance and immediately recognized him. He'd tried to avoid running into the man, but failed.

"Well, if it ain't my old lootenant!" Carson had blurted out when the two came face to face at the door to the telegraph office the second day after Carson's arrival. "I hope to hell you aren't in charge *here*. All that stink you stirred up about me at Hartsuff kept me from getting the Medal of Honor. Cost me a damned good job as a front man for a big livestock company when I got discharged."

"You look like you're doing pretty well to me," Coyle had replied evenly. The man's black hair was growing over his collar, and he hadn't shaved in a day or two. He also looked thinner than Coyle remembered him, and he walked with a slight limp, possibly from the old leg injury.

"Scrabbling for a story here and there as a reporter for the *Omaha Bee*? Not what you'd call high living. They don't pay reporters worth a damn."

"Too bad." Coyle had had to bite his tongue, remembering how Carson had gloated over his court-martial and dishonorable discharge. "Get out of my way." He shoved past Carson.

Where was Carson today? Since Coyle was now acting Pine Ridge agent, he had the authority to order anyone off the reservation who was not there on official government business. But the working policy had been to allow reporters, even though they were denied use of the agency telegraph to file their stories. And, so far, Coyle had no real justification. He wished he could get rid of *all* reporters, since most of their scare stories were aggravating what was essentially a peaceful situation. The provocative headlines were having an adverse affect on the Sioux, especially since many of them could read English and had access to newspapers that were shipped to Rushville and brought to the reservations with other supplies.

He was just refiling the letters, when the door opened, and Molly Seeker came in.

"Well, this is a surprise," he greeted her. "It's always a pleasure to see you, but what are you doing out of school?"

"So many of the Indian parents have come and taken their children out of school that we really have one teacher too many, so we're taking turns giving each other a day off."

"Great. I'm hungry. If you're free for lunch, may I recommend Dawson's store? I hear the cuisine there is delightful."

She gave a mock curtsy and offered him her arm. "Thank you, kind sir. I'd love to. Besides," she continued in her normal tone, "unless we cook for ourselves, we don't have a lot of choice."

He wondered what there was about this woman that attracted him. He tried to analyze it as they sat opposite each other, eating bowls of steaming beef stew. She was a rather ordinary-looking woman, her fair skin prematurely weathered from this dry climate, tiny crow's feet at the corners of her eyes. Maybe it was her open, self-assured mien. He had no sense of tension with her. She actually seemed interested in what he had to say. There was no verbal sparring, such as he'd experienced with other women. He thought she would probably make a better agent than Royer. At least, she had more experience with the Sioux.

Coyle had avoided making close friends of any of the other employees at this agency since he assumed he would be here less than a month. But he'd come in August and now it was November, and there was as yet no end in sight.

"I'm sorry. What did you say?" he asked, realizing she was looking at him expectantly and had been saying something.

"You've been separated from your family for quite a spell."

"Yes," he replied, wondering if this was an oblique way of asking if he was married. Nearly all of their previous conversations had dealt with their respective jobs, the new agent, and the situation on the reservation. For their own individual reasons, neither of them had yet probed into anything personal.

"I haven't seen my wife and two kids for five years," he replied carefully, studying her face for a reaction. The blue eyes held only polite interest. "I usually work out of Washington, and they live in southern Illinois."

The obvious question hung in the air between them — the *why* she was too courteous to voice. It was the same question Coyle had been grappling with for five years.

Chapter Ten

November 20, 1890
Pine Ridge Agency

Thad Coyle was wide awake and irritated that he couldn't go back to sleep. He'd awakened a short time earlier in the darkness and had fumbled his way, shivering in his long johns, out the back door of the agent's house to the privy. The half moon had set, and the blackness was nearly total except for a yellow square of light shining from a window of the telegraph office that was manned around the clock. As he held his breath in the stench of the outhouse, he estimated the temperature was still somewhere around fifty degrees outside — unusually mild for a November night in the Dakotas.

Back in bed now, he rolled into a more comfortable position and debated whether to strike a match and look at his watch on the small bedside table. He decided to wait a few minutes. Maybe he'd doze off again. But events of the past several days began to churn through his mind, and he knew from experience that sleep was done for the night.

Only five days ago a telegram had arrived with the message he'd been dreading:

> The President has directed the Secretary of War to assume a military responsibility for the suppression of any threatened outbreak among the Indians.

Agent Royer had returned from Rushville the following day, Saturday, to find that his frantic cries for help had finally prompted this action. He was a changed man, exuding confidence to the point of cockiness, swaggering around the office, thumbs hooked in his vest pockets, reminding Coyle of a banty rooster surveying his hen house. Disgusted with this performance, Coyle had begun looking for reasons to stay out of his sight. He had walked among the buildings of the agency, stopping at the traders' stores, the telegraph office, talking quietly with one or two of the agency police. He had sought out the company of Molly Seeker when she wasn't busy, and they had spent several hours in conversation over coffee in the kitchen of the agent's house. He'd gotten past his earlier embarrassment at having confided too much of his private life to a woman he'd only recently met. He had certainly not intended to divulge to her the details of his court-martial and his relationship with his wife. Perhaps it was just Molly's skills as a teacher that had elicited from him things long past, but hardly forgotten. He had not been conscious of her probing or prying. She was just a damnably easy woman to talk to.

More telegrams had arrived in the past days, informing Royer that troops were being sent to occupy Pine Ridge. The agent had taken his buggy and gone south to Rushville again to meet them.

Finally, giving up any attempt to sleep, Coyle rose and pulled on his clothes, then went into the kitchen and lighted the oil lamp on the table. It was ten minutes past four. He groaned and rubbed his eyes. He wasn't sleepy; he was just plain tired. Worry had not been part of his life for a long time. Instead, concern, thinking ahead, trying to anticipate and plan had become his habit. He only wished there were someone here to share his thoughts with. To his surprise, he thought of Emma, rather than Molly Seeker. Emma lived in Cairo, Illinois now, and operated a small bakery out of her sister's home. His daughter Jill was eighteen, and his son Brad twenty. It hardly seemed possible. Where had the time gone?

He swallowed some cold coffee left in the pot and tore off a hunk of bread to munch on as he slipped into his corduroy coat, and put on his hat. The darkness was better suited for thinking, and he felt like walking.

He was nearly at the south end of the deserted agency main street when he heard the first sounds of approaching wagons, the soft thudding of many hoofs, and the jingle of trace chains. He strained his eyes but felt, rather than saw, the movements of the troops approaching from the south. He stopped next to a wooden building to listen and wait. The muffled commands of non-coms reached his ears and the soft shuffling of many feet. Infantry. Not enough horses to be all cavalry, he decided. They'd made a night march from the railroad at Rushville. He walked silently closer and for the next half hour watched, by means of several lanterns moving about, the white, pointed Sibley tents blossom in rows as the Army set up camp south and west of the agency. Very smart, to slide in three hours before dawn and get deployed before any of the unsuspecting Indians camped around the agency were aware of their presence. Some commander was to be congratulated for using his head. If the troops had arrived during daylight hours, many of the Sioux would have panicked and fled at the sight of so many blue coats approaching with their wagons of supplies, as if they intended to stay. Although he

149

couldn't see them, Coyle guessed the Army had brought some intimidating fire power in the form of Hotchkiss guns that would be deployed on the low hills to the west and have a clear sweep of the Indian encampments. Yet, the Lakotas camped here were not the ones doing the dancing and creating all the disturbance. These were the ones who had come into the agency to show their good intentions.

A few minutes later Coyle heard the *clopping* of a single horse, coming up the street, and a buggy pulled up in front of the agent's house he'd just vacated. Of course, he thought — it was Royer, returning with the troops, undoubtedly as proud as Cæsar reëntering Rome at the head of his legions.

He guessed it was well past five o'clock, but as yet there was no hint of dawn. He'd given up smoking years before, but now he wished he had the comfort of an old briar pipe packed with rough-cut tobacco. He sighed, and turned up the collar of his jacket as a pre-dawn breeze chilled the back of his neck. Tobacco was like many other things in life, including alcohol and women, he reflected — an attraction that, indulged in often enough, became an addiction.

He crossed the street diagonally to the agency offices and let himself in with his key. He lighted the lamp on the desk and turned the wick low to keep from blinding himself. If the commanding officer wanted to report that his troops were deployed, the light would let him know that someone was up and stirring. The Army was not responsible for reporting to any civilian agent. Royer had seen to that. And he was probably already in his bed. But at least Coyle would keep the office available the rest of the night hours.

Molly Seeker joined Coyle in the office just as full daylight illuminated the drab Pine Ridge buildings.

"Well, for better or for worse, they're here," she said with no preliminaries as she shut the door behind her. She was hatless but had a knit shawl wrapped tightly around her narrow shoulders.

He nodded. "Quite a sight, huh?"

"I can't picture you as ever being a part of that," she said, her distaste creeping into her voice. "I give you credit for being a much more independent thinker."

"Well, I *was* part of that for many years," he said, feeling obliged to defend his former way of life. "It's something you get used to, taking orders. In a way, it's a secure life . . . regular pay, clothes, and a bed and a horse provided. Food and someone to cook it . . . all furnished at no cost."

"If it was so good, why didn't you stay?"

He looked at her and silently shook his head. They both knew the answer to that. "School today?" he inquired, noting she was not dressed with her usual care, and her blonde hair was not done up, but only pulled back away from her face with a hair band.

"No. School's out the rest of the week. The children are too upset to learn anything just now. All we can hope to do is keep them distracted until this blows over. I have a feeling Royer will have to order the tribal police to prevent the parents from pulling their children out. The schoolhouse could become a fortress."

"A General Brooke is in command of these troops. He came in here about an hour ago, and I met him. Middle-aged, portly, conservative. Seems like a man with a head on his shoulders. He told me he has five companies of infantry and three of cavalry. The cavalry is the Ninth . . . all buffalo soldiers. I told him that, even with a total of about three hundred and seventy men, two Hotchkiss guns and a Gatling gun, he's still considerably outnumbered and outgunned just by the Indians who are already camped around this agency. But he's under strict orders from General Miles to keep his men away from the Indians. The Army is just here to make a show of force for those Lakotas who may be inclined to start trouble."

"These Indians have been selling their horses and wagons and everything else of value to buy rifles and ammunition," Molly said. "I know for a fact that they have hundreds of repeating Winchesters."

Coyle nodded. "Not a good situation. I'm afraid our friend, Royer, has just brought the torch closer to the powder keg."

Chapter Eleven

November 27, 1890
Pine Ridge Agency

"Now that Royer's authority is bolstered by troops, I'll probably be recalled to Washington soon," Coyle remarked to Molly Seeker a week later. They were in the agency offices alone. Royer had gone home for lunch.

Her eyebrows arched in surprise. "You really think everything's under control?"

Coyle shrugged. "Maybe. Maybe not. But now that the Seventh cavalry has arrived from Fort Riley, the Army's got a good grip around this agency no matter what happens. I'm extra baggage here now."

"I think we need someone with common sense and experience more than ever," she said, rolling a fresh sheet of paper into her typewriter and adjusting the carbon, "what with Royer acting like a king, and all these nervous recruits who've never even seen an Indian before."

"The officers and non-coms will hold them

in check," Coyle replied calmly.

"I wish I could say the same for the Lakota leaders. They can try persuasion on their young bucks and the hysterical ghost dancers, but any little thing could set them off."

"As soon as he got here, General Brooke sent out riders to every camp and village on the reservation with the message that he wanted them all to come in and camp at this agency," Coyle said.

"Why?"

"He claims it's so his soldiers can protect them easier. From exactly *what* I don't know. But I suspect the real reason is so he can separate the dancers . . . who won't come in . . . from all the others who aren't following the new religion."

"What if they refuse to come?" Molly asked. "Most of them are very leery of being close to the blue coats."

"Their rations will be cut off."

"Very persuasive," she remarked.

"It's really stirring up a reaction," Coyle said. "General Brooke was in the office yesterday and showed me and Royer a message he'd just received from Little Wound. That band says the government can keep its rations since they amount to so little, anyway. Little Wound and his followers intend to keep dancing until spring. If the Messiah doesn't show up then, they'll stop." He shook his head. "This whole ghost dance scare will die out in a few months."

"It won't die out as long as the reporters are here. Look at these." She picked up copies of several newspapers that had just been delivered with the supplies from Rushville.

GETTING READY TO FIGHT the *Chicago Daily Tribune* blared. **ON THE EVE OF A BATTLE** the *New York Times* declared. **THE INDIANS MASSING FOR A STAND AGAINST THE TROOPS.** The *Omaha Bee* reported: **REDSKINS WITH GUNS ARE DANCING THE DREADED GHOST DANCE. GREAT EXCITEMENT AT THE PINE RIDGE AGENCY.**

Coyle looked down the page and saw the by-line of Thomas Carson. He read down the column:

People are just at the point today where the firing of a gun would undoubtedly precipitate a fight to the finish. The chances for blood and trouble here are very good today as they have been for several days. As a correspondent on the spot, I propose to continue to warn the public that there is grave danger from many thousands of Indians at Pine Ridge Agency. Will we ever get out of this with our hair?

The article continued in the same vein, but Coyle tossed it aside with a disgusted snort.

"The *Rapid City Journal* says . . . 'Everything was quiet today at the agency and no trouble was expected,' " Molly read aloud. "And the *Chadron Advocate* says . . . 'There was peace at Pine Ridge, whatever might be at the homes of frightened settlers and in the great newspaper offices.' "

"The problem is those last two are small papers with limited circulation," Coyle said. "Not many people are going to see or heed their calm voice of reason. It's the Chicago and Omaha and New York papers that will get the majority all stirred up." He picked up a copy of the *Sturgis Weekly Record*. "Unfortunately not many folks will read this . . . 'It is a well-known fact that Indians have been buying cartridges wherever they could for the last ten years. They all have guns, and they love to shoot. Firing off a gun is about the greatest form of dissipation they are acquainted with. Yet the mere fact of one of them asking for a cartridge is accepted as red-eyed proof of murder. It would pay the Immigration Department of South Dakota to lynch the majority of these liars and stand the expense. This ghost dance has been worked up into a very wonderful and exciting matter by pin-headed "war correspondents" and other irresponsible parties until they have succeeded in massing nearly half the United States Army to be spectators to an Indian powwow.' "

Coyle laughed. "I think he's hit the problem dead center. But a rural weekly newspaper isn't going to change anybody's mind. Unfortunately, in any place or time, blood and thunder will sell more papers than calm and reasonable explanations about peace."

"Do you know about this so-called 'news factory' that's operating out of the back room of the Asay brothers' store?" she asked.

He nodded. "I expect that's where my *old friend,* Tom Carson, is getting most of the stuff he's writing."

"Is there any way you or Royer can break that up, or order those people off the reservation?"

He shook his head. "I'm afraid that would just smack of censorship, and give more credence to the sensationalism they've been writing. Besides, some of those local mixed-bloods and squawmen who've been scraping up all the tidbits of gossip and rumor and processing them into saleable *news* articles for the journalists have a right to be on the reservation. They live here."

"Those men are troublemakers here even when things are normal," she remarked disgustedly. "Ott Means, Nick Janis, Dick

Middleton, and Don Nelson. And the reporters have hired Tim Crimmins to carry their dispatches to the telegraph office at Rushville, so the more trips he makes, the more money he earns. Why don't you go over there and hang around a while? Your presence might put a damper on some of that."

He considered it. "That's Royer's job."

"They have no fear of Royer."

"Royer threw one man off the reservation for calling him an ineffective coward in print," Coyle said. "I guess even a coward can get forceful when it comes to his own pride and reputation."

She silently continued to read some of the news stories. "Maybe I should leave here and get a teaching job some place else," she mused.

He felt an unexpected twinge of regret at her remark. "You're not thinking of quitting right away, are you?"

She shook her head. "No. I have a contract from year to year. Besides, I wouldn't leave them in the middle of the school term, even though we're more caretakers than teachers just now."

Why, he wondered, was he so relieved that she was not going? Was it because he would lose the only confidant he had at the agency? Or was it something more?

"Do you think your bosses will recall you soon?" she asked.

"I hope not." He moved across the room and opened the door of the potbelly stove, stirring up the fire with a poker, then shoving in two more dry pieces of split firewood. "Maybe they'll let me stay until this ghost dance issue resolves itself. If this weather keeps up, I expect it will be over by Christmas or the first of the year."

A gust of wind shook the frame building and rattled sleet against the glass windows. Even with the stove going full blast, there was a decided chill in the room when one moved more than six feet from the stove. At the moment, there was no snow, but that situation threatened to change as a blast of Canadian air drove low, dark clouds in from the north.

"I think I *will* take a hike over to the Asays' store," he remarked, reaching for his coat. "There's always a card game going on there, and I could use a drink." He could tell from her grateful look that he was not fooling her about the purpose of his visit.

He glanced out the window and saw Royer's gray derby and overcoat approaching. "Want to go along?" he asked.

"No. I'm a little tired. As soon as I finish typing this letter for Royer, I'm going home to read or take a nap." She looked at him with a twinkle in her blue eyes. "If anything exciting happens, I'm sure I'll hear about it quickly enough."

Coyle ducked his head against the stinging particles of ice as he crossed the street. He tried to plan what his attitude would be when he encountered Carson again. There was something about the presence of the man that brought back vivid memories of his Army days. Anger he thought he'd suppressed long ago came flooding back to inflict sharp stabs of pain and regret. What if he had held his temper that April day fourteen years ago or gone along and added his name to the lies on the Medal of Honor recommendation? He would probably have finished his career and retired as a captain with a small pension and wouldn't have to be totally dependent on his current salary. But, even as these thoughts troubled him, he knew he had made the right choice. What a price he'd paid for his self-esteem! The only thing that bothered him at this late date was the nagging doubt that he could have somehow resolved that whole issue without a direct confrontation. If he had been more diplomatic, he possibly could have saved both his career *and* his honor.

Ambition had never attacked him with its fatal sting. He had wanted only to get by, to

161

get along, to make a reasonable living without too much fuss and no notoriety. It was probably for this reason that the sight of Thomas Carson so infuriated him because it brought up images of a past he could not change. It was an irrational anger, but he vowed it would not master him as it had in years past.

As he entered the back room of the Asays' store, the cold air from outside swirled the cigar smoke that hung in a layer near the ceiling. Several men looked up curiously when he entered, but went back to their card game. A single, two-foot square window, set high on the side wall, admitted the only gray light from outside. A Rochester lamp hung from the ceiling to provide illumination for the card players. Three of the reporters, who'd been unable to find rooms or sleeping accommodations elsewhere, were rolled up in their blankets on the wooden floor along the walls, sound asleep. He wondered if the others were ensconced in the roomier spaces of trader James Finlay's store and post office. The reporters had laughingly dubbed the place the Hotel de Finlay.

Coyle suspected the liquor had been flowing, even this early in the day. On one side of the room Ott Means and Tim Crimmins sat at a table, poring over several sheets of paper. The news factory was in full operation. He stepped to the small makeshift bar and ordered beer. The man on duty drew off a mug of draft from a wooden keg and set it before him. Coyle laid down a quarter in payment and scanned the faces in the room as his eyes grew accustomed to the dimness. A feeling of relief went over him when he saw that Thomas Carson was not there. It was too much to hope that he'd gotten bored and gone back to Omaha.

"Seen Carson around?" he asked the bartender who'd resumed reading his newspaper.

"Hasn't been in today. He hired a horse and packed off that camera somewhere early this morning. I saw him riding out north as I was coming to work."

Coyle stiffened. "Was he alone?"

"Yeah."

"You don't know where he was going?"

"He never said," the barkeep replied. He smoothed the corners of his mustache with the back of his hand. "A few of the boys was discussin' the ghost dance in here last night. I recollect some of them askin' why Carson didn't try to get a picture of one as long as he had that big bulky camera with him."

Pretending disinterest, Coyle sipped his beer and stared around the room as the bartender went back to reading. Then he drained his mug, grabbed his hat, and went out through the back door and started for the employees' quarters where Molly had a room.

He rapped on the door and Molly opened it, her finger inserted between the pages of a book.

"Can I borrow your horse?" he asked.

"Certainly. Where're you going?"

"I think Carson will try to photograph a ghost dance. I need to find him and stop him before he causes trouble or maybe gets himself killed."

"This is the same man who caused you to be court-martialed?"

"Indirectly."

"Why do you care what happens to him? If he tends to rush out onto thin ice, let him take the consequences." She didn't sound bitter — only practical.

"I'm not concerned about him. I'm just afraid he'll set off some bigger disturbance that will engulf us all."

"I know the reservation better than you do. I'll go with you."

"That's not a good idea."

"Where did Carson go?"

"The bartender said he rode north."

"Hmm. The nearest ghost dancing that I know of is at No Water's village on White

Clay Creek, about seventeen miles northwest of here."

He hesitated, wondering if this were something he had to do alone. He certainly didn't want to expose her to any danger. On the other hand, she might prove a valuable asset with her intimate knowledge of the land and the Sioux.

"We can't ride the same horse," he said.

"There's a buggy in the stable for the use of the agency employees," she said. "We can hitch my horse to that. I've used her in harness before."

"Get your coat and hat," he said. "We may already be too late. He left about three hours ago."

"Come in out of the cold a minute." She held open the door for him. "Should we tell Royer?"

"And give him something else to worry about? Not on your life."

In less than thirty minutes they were spinning away from the agency in the black buggy, following the faint tracks along the winding course of White Clay Creek. The windy, gray day put a damper on their conversation. Coyle sniffed snow on the air. With any luck, the Indians would not be dancing, and Carson would have made the trip for nothing. *If,* in fact, this was the village toward which Carson was heading.

After five miles, Molly offered to drive, and he handed her the reins. His fingers were cold inside his leather gloves, and, as he sat on his hands to warm them, he silently wished he had a pair of mittens instead.

It was several minutes past three by Coyle's watch when they topped a slight rise in the prairie and came in sight of a scattering of canvas lodges and four log cabins about a mile ahead. Coyle slitted his eyes against the north wind that was blowing into their faces and looked at the sky. Less than two hours to darkness on this gloomy November day. The wind brought the faint sounds of chanting.

With a light touch on the reins, Molly drew her horse to a stop. "What now?" she asked.

"Do you know any of this band?"

"Probably. I'll have to see. I would guess a few of their children are at the school. But if you're thinking I might have some influence with these dancers, you're wrong. They might even be resentful of me keeping their children against their will." Then she added: "Once religious fanatics of any culture get emotionally wrought up, nothing short of God or bullets can stop them."

Coyle nodded, thinking that maybe Carson had already gotten his photographs from a distance and was on his way back. But they hadn't passed him on the road. It would soon be too dark to get good pictures. "Let's go," he said. "We'll just play whatever cards we're dealt. If Carson's not around, I'll make up some excuse for us being here, and we'll make a quick exit."

Molly slapped the reins over the horse's back, and they started down the long, gradual incline toward the line of trees that marked the creek and the village. As they approached, they could see fires being kindled in the distance, apparently for light and warmth as the dancing continued into the evening. Coyle expected to encounter at least a couple of sentries, but no one challenged them. Out of habit he reached under his coat to the butt of his Remington in its holster. It gave him a feeling of security, even though he knew he would not use it except in case of dire emergency. With as many rifles as these Indians had, one pistol would be totally ineffective, anyway.

Molly reined up near the first cabin. About fifty yards away, the Indians were chanting in Lakota as the big circle of dancers shuffled left. Coyle saw several of them thrusting carbines over their heads.

Coyle drew a deep breath. He saw no sign of Carson. Now all he'd have to do was present a plausible excuse to three grim-visaged Sioux who were approaching.

"What do you want?" the bigger of the three demanded as they stopped a few feet from the buggy. All three held rifles.

"Have you seen a white man ride this way today?" Coyle asked.

"No whites." The Lakota glared at him.

"Let's go, Molly," Coyle said softly. He started to add — "We got lucky . . ." — but, before the words could be uttered, a scream, tempered by the wind sounded somewhere off to the left, followed by shouting in both English and Lakota.

The three Indians who confronted them suddenly turned and ran toward the commotion.

Coyle took the reins from Molly and pulled the horse around, snapping the lines. The buggy lurched forward.

"Carson!" he said tersely. "I've heard that voice often enough to know it."

There was a string of vile curses in English, and Coyle saw a knot of men about thirty yards from the dancers. He pulled the horse to a halt. "Stop!" he yelled at the top of his voice. He was ignored as he heard the sounds of splintering wood and saw the legs of a camera tripod flip into the air.

Carson was trying to struggle loose from

three Sioux who held his arms as he screeched every abusive name he could lay his tongue to. This stream of invective was abruptly cut short by the thrust of a rifle butt to his head. Carson dropped from view.

"Leave him alone!" Coyle yelled. He leaped out of the buggy. "I'm arresting this man! He's going to the Pine Ridge jail." He kept his hands in plain view as he slowly approached the small group who were now warily watching him. He made no sudden or overt moves as he saw hate in those flat, black eyes. They held their rifles at waist level. His heart was thudding so heavily in his chest he was sure they could see it shaking his frame. Indians usually did not have the discipline of trained troops. They always acted as individuals. If one of them decided to shoot, he would act on his own. Coyle hoped his words and calm demeanor would placate the Indians long enough to get the stunned and bleeding Carson into the buggy. "He will not take pictures of the ghost dance," Coyle continued, stating the obvious since the box camera lay smashed on the ground.

Coyle grabbed Carson by the coat collar and yanked him to his feet, pushing him toward the buggy. Blood streamed from a gash in the hairline where the brass butt plate of the carbine had struck him. Coyle knew scalp wounds bled freely, but was more concerned about a cracked skull as Carson wobbled and had to be held upright.

"So you're messin' with me again, Lootenant!" Carson spat blood at him. "You don't ever get enough, do you?"

"Get your ass in that buggy before I let them have you," Coyle hissed at him.

"Where's my horse?" Carson mumbled. As Molly reached to help him, he stumbled and fell over the front wheel.

"Never mind. We'll get it later."

"Don't want those damned Injuns to get my gear," he muttered groggily as he struggled into the buggy.

Hands in plain view, Coyle backed away and climbed aboard. Eight Lakotas silently followed him, saying nothing. Molly pulled the horse around and whipped the animal into motion.

Coyle didn't look back but had a strange feeling between his shoulder blades, anticipating that a lead slug might come slamming through the back of the buggy. But a hundred yards flowed past, and he began to relax. He reached into Carson's pocket and pulled out a bandanna and shoved it into the man's hand. "Wipe the blood off your face," he said, supporting the lean man between himself and Molly on the narrow seat. *Maybe now I can get this troublemaker expelled from the reservation,* he thought, staring ahead across the horse's back at the darkening landscape.

Chapter Twelve

November 28, 1890
Pine Ridge Agency

Perversely Thomas Carson quickly became a man to be admired and envied by his colleagues. With his wound stitched by Dr. Eastman and a white bandage wound about his head, he went around Pine Ridge Agency, accepting free drinks for repeating his story of blood and thunder. He cast himself as the central, courageous figure, fighting his way to safety through the armed Indians who had wantonly attacked him. Coyle overheard part of this story in the Asays' store where Carson was regaling some of his fellow reporters, and the news factory men.

"They got my horse, but I got away on foot and had to hoof it part way back to the agency. Ran into Agent Coyle and Miss Seeker who were out buggy riding. They gave me a ride back to the doctor."

Coyle tipped up his beer and drained it, feeling all eyes in the room swivel toward him.

"I reckon that tightwad of a boss of mine

172

will take the money for that camera out of my pay. Lucky I took some views around here before it got busted," Carson continued.

His listeners chuckled, and someone shoved another full beer in front of him.

Coyle ordered food and went to find a table. Twenty minutes later he was digging into his fried potatoes and salt pork when a familiar voice grated into his privacy.

"Ah, Lootenant" — Carson smirked — "the word around here is that you are a special Indian agent. Still working for the government." He moved a little closer and lowered his voice. "One might wonder just how you came to get such a high and mighty job, what with your background and all."

Coyle cringed inwardly. He should never have come into the Asays' store. But this agency was a small place, and, wherever he went, he was likely to run into Carson. He continued eating in silence.

"You might at least invite me to sit down."

Coyle motioned to the empty chair on the opposite side of the table. Carson hooked it out with a foot and sat down with his beer glass. "Hard for me to stand up too long at a stretch with my gimpy knee. You remember how that happened, don't you? Maybe with proper treatment it might have healed up better."

Coyle laid down his fork and looked directly at him. "What do you want me to do about it?"

"Not a thing," Carson replied. "I'm just reminding you of old debts. I happen to know that no soldier with a dishonorable discharge gets hired again by the U.S. government. So you either had a lot of pull with someone, or you lied on your application and got away with it. I'm thinking it was the latter."

"And . . . ?" Coyle had lost his appetite. He opened and closed his fists in his lap, fighting down the anger that was beginning to rise at the leering face across from him. "Make your point."

"No point. I'm just thinking that now I've got the upper hand. Since no Indian war has materialized, we're all a little hard up for news. I might just have to stir things up a bit by writing a piece for the *Omaha Bee* questioning how a man of violent temper with a dishonorable discharge from the Army happens to be on this reservation representing the Indian Bureau."

Coyle sat, tight-lipped.

Carson grinned widely. "Just keep that in mind." He rose from his chair. "I'll be looking for a little more respect from you, Lootenant. You might even offer to buy me a drink or a meal next time we meet, seeing as how you're probably pretty flush." He raised his beer glass in mock salute and limped away.

Disgusted, but silent, Coyle walked out of the store. That morning he'd strongly suggested to Royer that Carson be sent packing. But, to his surprise, the agent was reluctant to do so, thinking that such an action would only provoke more personal invective in the press, especially in the pages of the *Omaha Bee.*

"Why don't you stand up for yourself?" Molly Seeker complained, when she encountered Coyle coming out of the Asays' store and he relayed what Carson had said.

"I told Royer. That's enough," he replied, striding toward the agency offices.

She gave him a disgusted look. "You're just going to let him strut around here, crowing like a banty rooster? Most of these Indians know what he's saying . . . those that know English."

"Then they understand that his words are no truer than what he writes," Coyle replied, unruffled. "There's an old Arab proverb . . . 'Dogs bark, but the caravan moves on.' "

"You're saying that nothing he says or does is going to make any difference?"

"That's about it."

"I wish I could be as sure of that as you are."

He put his hand on her arm. "Nobody

175

knows the future, Molly. We just have to make the best decisions we can and trust things will work out. Word will get around among the Indians as to what exactly happened. I don't want to push my name as some kind of hero among the whites and the troops. If Carson wants to portray himself as a big man, let him. He knows what really happened, and I'm sure it infuriates him that we had to come to his rescue."

"Do you think they would have killed him?" Molly asked, as they stopped in front of the agency porch.

"Hard to say. In the heat of resentment and anger, they might have. Cool heads would have known it would only bring trouble from the troops if they'd killed a white man. But I didn't see any cool heads there last night."

Molly was silent for a moment. "I've worked here four years, and I thought I knew these people. I'm beginning to think that I don't really know them at all."

Coyle thought she looked distressed. "Is that the first time you've been near a ghost dance?"

"Yes."

"You're used to dealing with the children and some of the parents in a different setting. You see a completely different side of their lives."

"I know. I shouldn't expect them to all have the same attitudes and religions any more than I would a large group of whites. My life here has been relatively sheltered, even though I've traveled about the reservation some. I can see now why everyone's so disturbed about this ghost dance frenzy. Those dancers were acting crazy. And many of them were armed."

Without thinking, Coyle encircled her with his arms and hugged her close to him. "Don't worry, Molly. Everything will work out." He held her for several seconds, trying to impart some reassurance, before finally stepping back.

"Thanks." She gave him a tight smile, blinking away tears.

"You coming into the office?"

She shook her head. "I have to teach a class in thirty minutes." She smiled, then looked intently at him. "See you for supper, maybe? I'm fixing steak and potatoes tonight."

"I'll be there." He squeezed her hand, then turned away, and stepped up onto the porch.

Molly was still a bit shaken by their rescue of Carson. As she reflected on the violence that had scarcely been averted, her hand trembled slightly. She put down the hairbrush and continued looking at her reflection in the small, cracked mirror above the washstand. Not bad. But her fair skin was wind-burned, and she noticed some fine lines around her mouth and eyes. Age or the harsh Dakota climate — possibly both. She was long past the age when polite white society considered her a spinster. An old maid schoolteacher — something she would have shuddered at years ago.

She turned away to check the table. The agency dishes were chipped and didn't match, but it was the best she could do. She knew the steak and fried potatoes were good — and the homemade bread. Surely Coyle wouldn't be expecting anything fancy here.

What would Charles Eastman think? Her thoughts jumped to the second man who'd recently come into her life. She'd been introduced to the handsome young doctor only a couple of weeks before at a dinner given by the wife of one of the traders. They had hit it off immediately. She was very attracted to him. The only problem was his race — he was a full-blood Santee Sioux from Minnesota, even though he'd been reared in white culture and earned his M.D. degree from Boston University in the same city where she'd grown up. With her permission, he'd called on her twice since then, and she found him delightful company — thoroughly at home in both white and Lakota society. She wondered what her family in Boston would think of her possibly being courted by an Indian. They had thought her a little odd and adventurous for going off to teach school on a remote reservation. They even considered her a missionary, of sorts.

She angrily shook off the thought. Let them think what they would. Except physically, Eastman was as white as anyone she'd ever known — and much better educated. He was a charming man in all respects, able to converse on any subject. Besides, it was no one else's business but her own. She had to make her own life. She, of all her socialite girl friends, had had the courage to come west to teach Indians four years ago. True, her decision had come after most of her close friends and former classmates had married and were starting their own families. *Damn them!* she thought. She wouldn't let anyone else determine what she would do.

As for this handsome Thad Coyle — well, he was older, much experienced in the ways of the world. She was also very attracted to him. A wife somewhere was the only roach in the buttermilk. But she had never been one to worry about what might be. Drive ahead and deal with whatever came — that had always been her philosophy.

A rap at the door startled her out of her reverie. She pulled down the sleeves of her blouse and slipped off the apron over her head before opening the door.

"Don't *you* look nice," Coyle said, stepping inside. "And what is that delicious smell?"

Chapter Thirteen

December 2, 1890
Pine Ridge Agency

Coyle watched Daniel Royer's face harden into a frown as he pulled at his mustache. "You say Kicking Bear, Short Bull, and Two Strike have joined forces?"

Police Lt. Thunder Bear nodded. "They lead more than twelve hundred of the People."

"Where?"

"They are moving west toward the table-land — to the Stonghold, my men tell me." The deep-chested Indian policeman stood before Royer's desk and waited impassively for a response or further instructions.

In the intervening seconds of silence, Coyle tried to picture the three Indian ghost dance leaders the lieutenant had just named. Kicking Bear had an aggressive Roman nose and heavy lips that curled in a permanent sneer at all things white. A man of forty-one years, he had fought at Little Bighorn and Slim Buttes. Short Bull was Kicking Bear's brother-in-law, a sharp-featured man of forty-five, short in stature, but tall in reputation as a former warrior and medicine man. He was a kindly, generous man who was mistakenly thought to be weak by some military officers. Coyle wasn't familiar with Two Strike except through his name and reputation as a Non-progressive. He was apparently very vigorous for a man past seventy years of age.

"Kicking Bear invited Sitting Bull and Big Foot to join them at the Stronghold where they will all dance until the coming of the Messiah," Thunder Bear said.

"What is this Stronghold?" Royer asked, obviously uncomfortable that he didn't already know.

"In the Badlands to the west. On a high mesa. There is good grass and water."

"They plan to spend the winter there?" Royer asked.

Thunder Bear nodded. "This is the Moon of Popping Trees, but the People are prepared to suffer the cold and dance until the Messiah comes in the spring."

Coyle was familiar with the Stronghold from his many trips across the Badlands since 1876, but he held his silence. This was between the agent and his police lieutenant.

"Swift Hawk has returned to join Big

Foot's people," Thunder Bear continued.

Coyle gave a slight start at this. "Was he also called Tom Merritt?"

"He lived long with that name among the whites," the lieutenant replied.

"That's all," Royer said, waving his hand in dismissal. "Don't interfere with the movement of those dancers in any way. Just keep me posted on where they are."

"It will mean long rides of many miles for several of my men," Thunder Bear stated. "The weather is getting very cold. They will need buffalo coats."

"All right." Royer scribbled an order on a pad, tore off the sheet, and handed it to the blue-uniformed lieutenant. "You can draw six coats from the warehouse for now."

Thunder Bear turned and left without comment. Coyle felt the blast of cold air as the office door swung open and closed.

"Makes you wonder how they kept warm before the white man came along to provide for them," Royer grunted.

"They hunted their own buffalo and made their own clothing," Coyle said before he thought.

Royer gave him a hard look, but apparently couldn't decide if Coyle was criticizing him.

"Guess I'd better get word about this to General Brooke," Royer said, reaching for his overcoat on the hall tree. "I wish he had set up his headquarters here in the office instead of at my house."

As a former military officer, Coyle knew General Brooke had appropriated part of the agent's roomy quarters for the sake of privacy and to avoid any confusion over the order of authority now that the Army was occupying the reservation. Not that he had anything to fear in the way of competition from Royer who had practically begged the military to come in and take over. But now Royer was constantly relaying messages from his tribal police to the general.

"That place in the Badlands isn't called the Stronghold for nothing," Coyle remarked as Royer slipped his arms into the overcoat. "It's a plateau with steep sides several hundred feet high all around. It's maybe three miles long by a mile wide. Thunder Bear didn't tell you it's connected to another plateau by only a narrow neck of land, hardly wide enough for two wagons to pass abreast. It has two good springs of water, plenty of grass for the animals, and firewood growing in eroded gullies along the rim. The Army will have the devil's own time rooting them out of there if the ghost dancers don't want to surrender."

"Hmm. Well, I guess I'll just have to let General Brooke worry about that," Royer said, putting on his bowler and reaching for the doorknob. "I'll see you later."

Coyle stood looking out the window after he left. It was a gray day, and the wind whipped up the dust from the street, nearly obscuring a two-story frame house he could just see from where he stood. It was the house built by the government for chief Red Cloud. Coyle knew the Indian Bureau was not entirely altruistic in its gift. They wanted the wily old chief close by where the agent could keep an eye on him. Red Cloud lived there but, in good weather, chose to camp out in the front yard.

Red Cloud, on this reservation, and Sitting Bull, who lived in a cabin on a remote part of the Standing Rock reservation to the north, covertly encouraged their followers to defy whites and dance the ghost dance. Having dealt with whites longer, they were more subtle than the young braves in resisting change and clinging to the old ways.

On the other hand, Big Foot, leader of the Miniconjous, advocated peace and capitulation. Kicking Bear, born an Oglala, had married into the Miniconjou band by wedding the niece of old Big Foot. Coyle wondered how these two men of different generations and divergent views got along with each other. If there was some way of fostering dissension between them, it might further break down resistance and bring peace.

He knew that while most of the white settlers and traders did not want a full war to break out, neither did they want the Army to pack up and leave, since the influx of soldiers, reporters, and others provided a great surge to the local economy. His mind turned again to what Thunder Bear had just reported. It was hard to imagine his old friend and freighting partner, Tom Merritt, back on the reservation, and with Big Foot. Apparently he had gone back to his Lakota name of Swift Hawk. After all these years of making his own way in white civilization, what had brought him back here? Had he finally taken enough of the slurs and insults from white men that he would throw over his adopted way of life and come back to support his former Lakota band? Had he been converted to the ghost dance religion in hopes of an imminent second coming of the Messiah? Coyle had not seen Merritt in more than eight years. A man could change a lot in that length of time. Coyle certainly had. Basically he was the same person, but his circumstances had altered considerably. Perhaps something traumatic had happened to his old friend to drive him back to the reservation. He wished he could be with old Big Foot's band for a short time to talk with Tom.

Maybe he could learn the truth. Big Foot, chief of the Miniconjous, had for several years shown an inclination to make peace with the whites. He was a canny diplomat who, Coyle suspected, never had any great love for white men or their culture but had seen the futility of continued resistance. Several years before, the old man, along with several other chiefs, had been invited to Washington, D.C. to meet with the great white father, and to be impressed by the railroads and the cities of the East. Under the guise of friendship, the politicians hoped to intimidate the chiefs with the millions of whites and their vastly superior technology.

Consequently Big Foot had become a strong advocate of making peace with the invaders. To him, the Lakotas must either capitulate or cease to exist. It was a simple matter of survival.

Coyle stared at the walls of the empty office, frustrated that he had no power to change the course of events. He felt sure the Army would try to stop Kicking Bear and Short Bull from leading twelve hundred men, women, and children to the Stronghold, and this could provoke a clash. It depended on how diplomatic General Miles chose to be. And Miles was not even here to assess the situation. He had taken the train from Omaha to

Rapid City, some ninety miles from here. There he'd set up headquarters and issued his orders and received reports back by telegraph.

Big Foot was now an old man, and his influence was undoubtedly waning among his followers. From rumors Coyle'd heard, at least two younger men in his band were pulling the others in the direction of the ghost dance. As an outsider, Coyle could only guess what must be going on within Big Foot's band. Were they coming into the agency as ordered by the Army, or had they joined the large migration toward the Stronghold?

Chapter Fourteen

December 6, 1890
Pine Ridge Agency Offices

"Are your men going to attack the Stronghold?" Agent Daniel Royer inquired of General Brooke, forcing himself into a conversation from which the agent had so far been excluded.

The barrel-chested military officer scrubbed a hand over his face without replying immediately. Coyle wondered if the bags under the general's eyes indicated a recent lack of sleep or just too many years of active duty. Brooke's blue tunic was in need of a good brushing, and his gray hair stood out in spots from static electricity as he pulled off his fur cap.

"I think that's the only way we'll ever root them out of there," Brooke replied. He took a deep breath and exhaled. "But General Miles has a different idea. He's afraid we'd lose too many good men and maybe start a general war in the process. He wants to throw a big loop around the hostiles and just stand our ground until winter weather really sets in. He thinks that will take the fight and resistance out of them." He paused to pour himself a cup of coffee from a pot on the stove that was vainly trying to warm the agency offices.

Besides Royer and Brooke, those sitting and standing in the office were Coyle, Molly Seeker, Jack Red Cloud, and Father John Jutz — a gray-haired priest who was in charge of Holy Rosary Mission — known as the Drexel Mission — a few miles to the north.

"I've sent two groups of friendly Sioux up there to try to talk the dancers out, but the sentries fired over their heads and drove them off," Brooke continued, sipping at the steaming cup. "Since I must follow orders, I'm deploying troops to the north and west to stand by. Miss Seeker and others tell me that Father Jutz, here, is highly respected by all the Lakotas as a man of his word." He nodded toward the elderly priest who made no comment. "I want Father Jutz and Jack Red Cloud to travel to the Stronghold and attempt to negotiate a surrender."

There was silence in the room as Coyle and the others stared at the general. It was an audacious plan, Coyle thought, that would require not only a stout heart but also endurance from the seventy-year old cleric, since the eighty-mile round trip would have to be made in a wagon or buggy, and the weather showed signs of turning nasty.

Coyle glanced sideways at the smooth, bronze face of Jack Red Cloud. Could this man be trusted? Only recently he'd been a staunch advocate of the ghost dance religion. What had made him suddenly switch sides and declare himself for appeasement and surrender? Coyle had no way of knowing what was in his mind, but maybe the Indian could convince the others to give up the new religion and come in peacefully.

Molly Seeker finally broke the silence. "Do you think it will work?"

"I'm gambling the dancers will think enough of Father Jutz at least to let him get in and talk to them. Jack Red Cloud will go along to help on the trip and to smooth out any interpretations with the language."

Coyle had heard the priest speak to some of the Indians in their native tongue. But Molly said the old man had not become completely fluent during the two years since he'd arrived to establish the Holy Rosary Mission and school.

"That's my idea. It'll be a hard, dangerous trip, Father, and you're perfectly free to refuse. I have no way of knowing whether your going would be any more successful than sending those friendly Indians who were driven off with gunfire."

191

"Of course, I'll go," the priest replied without hesitation. "I don't know if they'll listen to me, but if you think it might help, I'll try."

"That's what I was hoping you'd say," General Brooke said. "Jack Red Cloud will accompany you, and I think a third person representing the authority of the government should go along as an observer and to advise you on any matters pertaining to what the Indians can expect if they surrender . . . or, if they don't." He turned to Agent Royer, who quickly busied himself shuffling some papers on his desk. Then Brooke looked directly at Coyle. "My thought is to send Thaddeus Coyle. You're detailed here as Special Indian Agent out of Washington, and you have authority to act on behalf of the Indian Bureau. And I'll delegate military authority to carry our message."

Coyle's stomach tensed, and he looked across at Molly whose eyes were on him. "Be glad to," he replied shortly. "Anything that might get this whole mess resolved a little quicker." It wouldn't be a pleasant trip, he knew, but it beat sitting around the agency, waiting for something to happen. He would miss Molly's company, but at least he wouldn't have to look at Royer for a time, or his old nemesis, Carson.

"Then it's settled," Brooke said with obvious satisfaction. "You'll need a little time to prepare, but the sooner you're on the road, the better. By noon tomorrow at the latest."

That afternoon Coyle laid out his warmest clothing, including wool socks, cotton long johns, and corduroy pants, lined leather gloves, woolen muffler, and broad-brimmed felt hat. He would wear his revolver strapped to his waist, just in case, although he had no doubt he'd be disarmed before any talks took place.

Molly rapped at the open doorway of his room at the agent's house while he was filling his cartridge belt from a box on a shelf.

"Just wanted to invite you to a last home-cooked meal . . . steak." She smiled when he looked up. "It'll be a few days before you get anything better than dog or horsemeat."

"Word is the dancers have herded some stolen beeves up to the Stronghold to see them through the winter."

"You think they're going to share any of that meat with you?"

He grinned. "A steak in the hand. . . ."

"You're not wearing that old, threadbare wool coat, are you?" she asked, frowning.

"It's all I have."

"I've got a better one you can have."

"Belong to one of your former suitors?" He instantly regretted his words, even though he had meant it as a joke.

She gave him a disgusted look. "It's a buffalo coat that's too big for me. A Lakota woman gave it to me after her husband died. I did a few favors for her and her children. And don't worry, it's fairly clean," she added at his look of distaste. "At least no mange or lice."

He could see her biting her cheeks to keep from laughing. "If I like it, I'll buy it from you."

"We'll negotiate," she said, a mischievous twinkle in her blue eyes.

"I wish you were going," Coyle said to Molly as he stood on her porch in the windy darkness at eleven that night.

"And I wish you were staying. But neither one of us came to this god-forsaken country because it was safe and warm and comfortable."

The light from her open door was back-lighting her, forming a golden halo of blonde hair.

"You're right. Maybe someday we'll both be able to retire to some jobs that are safe and sane."

"Think how boring that would be," she said, grabbing him by the thick, fur collar of the buffalo coat and pulling him closer. "Oooh, it's cold out here!"

He opened the coat and pulled her inside, hugging her close. "You're warmer than this buffalo hide," he said huskily. "Maybe you should go with me."

"Mister Thaddeus Coyle" — she pronounced his name in mock seriousness, pulling back and looking up into his face in the yellow lamplight — "I want you out there on that windy prairie remembering this moment, and how you're warm and full of steak and homemade bread. But, mostly, I want you to think of me." She took his cold cheeks in the palms of her warm hands and kissed him soundly on the mouth. His heart was pounding as he hugged her one last time.

"Should be back in three or four days," he said, finally disengaging himself from her.

"Be careful," she said.

"Don't worry," he said, backing away and going down the steps to the dusty street. He strode away, and the light was blotted out as she closed the door behind him.

Just before noon the next day Father Jutz climbed onto the seat of the wagon beside Jack Red Cloud who held the reins of the mule team. Coyle settled himself in back, propped against the bedrolls. The Indian

195

snapped the lines over the backs of the team, and the light wagon rattled away down the frozen street. Coyle waved to Molly as she and Royer grew smaller on the porch. Then the figures disappeared in a sudden gust of snowflakes. It hardly seemed like high noon, Coyle reflected, huddling down in the collar of the buffalo coat. The low overcast and snow squalls created a twilight.

Earlier that morning, the thermometer on the porch of the agent's house had read zero. It had warmed up some since, but the temperature was still well below freezing. Or was it just the biting, high plains wind that made it seem so? A few minutes later they got a slight reprieve as Jack Red Cloud guided the mules down the White Clay Creek road, and they turned northwest so the wind was at their backs.

It was forty miles to the south wall of the Cuny Table, the plateau on which the Stronghold was located. At half past four by Coyle's watch, early winter darkness and blowing snow forced them to seek the partial shelter of a frozen creekbed to camp. After the mules had been unhitched and hobbled, Coyle helped the Indian slip feedbags of grain on the animals. The men chewed on beef jerky and hard bread, not attempting to gather any dead brush for a fire. The wind, the cold, and the darkness kept conversation to a minimum. The three men were traveling together on a common mission, but they might as well have been three strangers, as each sought his bedroll soon after dark. The priest found a clump of brush just below the lip of the cut bank, and Jack Red Cloud bedded down in the back of the wagon. Coyle crawled under the wagon, fully dressed including the buffalo coat, wrapping himself in his ground cloth. He wished for the insulating warmth of about two feet of dry snow, but bursts of wind were scouring the ground clear, scattering snow before the flakes could begin to collect. Coyle slept only fitfully, vaguely conscious of the cold seeping inside his boots.

The snow had stopped and a brittle blue sky and moderated wind greeted them when they rolled out, stiff and sore, at dawn. They hurried to hitch up the mules and be on their way.

It was late afternoon before they approached the Cuny Table and were met by mounted pickets armed with Winchesters. Two of the guards rode out to meet them, rifle barrels poking out from the blankets wrapped around their shoulders.

Jack Red Cloud pulled the mules to a halt and conversed with the riders in their common language. Apparently Father Jutz understood some of what was being said but made only one or two comments. The pickets whirled their mounts and rode away. Coyle expected to follow, but Jack Red Cloud turned to them with a disgusted look on his face. "They will ride to the Stronghold and ask permission for us to come in. But it's another ten miles there and ten back, so we might as well unhitch the mules and water them."

"These old bones have really stiffened up in the last thirty hours," Father Jutz said, climbing down and stretching.

"I know what you mean." Coyle nodded, thinking that he was probably just as cold and stiff, even though he was more than twenty years younger than the priest. Coyle helped with the mules, then jogged up and down to get his blood circulating and ward off the chill. The sun had retreated behind another cover of high clouds, making the wind-swept prairie and the edge of the broken Badlands seem even bleaker.

The pickets finally returned about three hours after dark and told Jack Red Cloud they could proceed. One of the pickets rode ahead to guide the way up the faint trail to the top of the plateau. Coyle clung to the sideboard of the jolting, sliding wagon as Jack Red Cloud urged the mules upward. To keep his mind off the likelihood of their going over the edge, he pondered his reasons for coming along on this mission. Dealing with Indians of any tribe, he'd discovered, was like dealing with petulant, prideful children. Their answers, decisions, and actions were often irrational — more whim than reasoned strategy. He'd learned from parlaying with the various Apache bands in Arizona Territory that any kind of negotiations could be very frustrating.

It was eleven o'clock that night before they finally rolled across the narrow land bridge and entered the Stronghold proper. The three visitors were guided to the tent of Short Bull, showing dully in the moonlight. Inside the big tent that was lighted and warmed with a small fire, Coyle recognized the heavy features of Short Bull. The Sioux dance leader sent a runner to bring Kicking Bear, Two Strike, Turning Bear, High Hawk, Crow Dog, Eagle Pipe, and several other whose names Coyle didn't know.

They all crowded into the tent, and the conference commenced. *By any standard, that Kicking Bear is a damned ugly man,* Coyle thought as he shed his buffalo coat in the fetid atmosphere of the big tent. The gusting wind sucked the walls of the tent in and out, draw-ing a small portion of the smoke from the fire ring out the hole in the top of the tent. Coyle sat cross-legged on a blanket, only half hearing the guttural harangues of the Lakota leaders. His fatigue, the close air, the smell of the oiled bodies, the slitted eyes — all seemed to press in on him. He caught himself fading in and out, hearing only a droning of words. In intervals of wakefulness, he was aware that most of the talking consisted of the ghost dance leaders enumerating their various grievances at the way they'd been treated by their white masters. They expressed anger over the census that cut 2,000 from the head count at the reservation, resulting in a corresponding cut in the food allowance. They objected to the new boundary between the Rosebud and Pine Ridge reservations that effectively separated many related members of the same band. They protested that their rations were somehow being stolen. Coyle realized that most of their complaints were true. Even though Father Jutz was somewhat conversant in the Lakota tongue and addressed the leaders directly, the longer harangues had to be translated by Jack Red Cloud. This prolonged the conference. Every time Father Jutz got a chance to speak, he pleaded with them to surrender. Even though they apparently had great respect for the old priest, Short Bull and Kicking Bear repeat-

edly rejected his requests for them to surrender. Because of their actions, Kicking Bear
said, each of the dance leaders was marked by
the authorities for arrest and confinement in
the white man's iron prison. They vowed to
stay and dance until spring, and to die fighting, if necessary, to protect their beliefs, when
the soldiers came. Coyle could sense they felt
time was on their side, that their dancing
would produce the appearance of the Messiah. "If He does not come by the time the
grass is thick, we will come in."

After hours of talking, nothing had been decided. Coyle's smoke-irritated eyes were crying for sleep, and he could imagine how the
seventy-year-old priest felt, since he'd been
actively negotiating the entire night and had
been without sleep for at least twenty-four
hours.

Yet, as daylight stole over the plateau, the
priest's calm persistence finally paid off. In
one of those inexplicable turnabouts, several
of the leaders suddenly announced they
would come in to the agency to talk with General Brooke. Coyle would never have thought
their recalcitrance would break, but, once the
decision was made, they set off immediately.
The delegation consisted of Two Strike,
Turning Bear, Big Turkey, High Pine, Big
Bad Horse, and Bull Dog, along with an es-

cort of two dozen armed warriors. War paint smeared their faces and arms, and eagles feathers fluttered from their hair and the manes and tails of their horses. Several of the men wore ghost shirts.

The party began the long, cold ride to the agency. Part of the time, Two Strike drove the mules of the wagon and rode with Father Jutz.

On the night of December 5th, they camped at the Holy Rosary Mission, and Coyle slept like a dead man, oblivious to the cold. The next morning they rode in to Pine Ridge Agency. The painted and feathered warriors rode proudly, most of them carrying repeating rifles. But Coyle noticed they hesitated and nearly bolted several times when they saw other riders. Jack Red Cloud said the dancers were afraid of treachery, especially since there were more than a thousand soldiers at the agency.

But they finally conquered their fear and rode in to Pine Ridge, heads held high, and dismounted in front of the agency office building. The chiefs crowded into the office in a semicircle, facing General Brooke and Colonels Wheaton and Forsyth.

Coyle slipped out as the talks began, knowing what was going to be said, and deciding he'd heard most of it before. When he returned with Molly nearly two hours later, the talk was just breaking up. Father John Jutz was rubbing his puffy eyes as he emerged onto the porch. "Nothing firm," he told Coyle and Molly. "Brooke's got them to thinking about the comforts of the agency. I think they might bring their people in. The ghost dance will be prohibited, of course. The chiefs pointed out there's not enough grass around here to feed their stock. The government will have to let them spread out and camp. But the main inducement is food. Brooke promised they'd all have enough to eat. And to back up that claim, he's having some beeves killed and a feast prepared right now. Everyone on the agency is invited. South of the corrals in about an hour."

"You think that will persuade them?" Coyle asked, taking Molly's arm and falling into step with the priest.

Jutz nodded, his gray hair flying in the breeze. "That, and the promise of the government not to punish anyone for plundering agency supplies or killing stock. God knows, the agents have done enough of that themselves," he added as an afterthought.

Everyone feasted that afternoon. Coyle and Molly joined in the festivities, and ate with the indefatigable Father Jutz.

"Besides fulfilling the government's promise to supply adequate food," the priest said, "Brooke told them that more of their young men would be hired as tribal policemen."

"Once all this ghost dance business settles down, I wonder what they'll police?" Coyle remarked.

"That's what Two Strike wanted to know," the priest answered. "But he seemed glad they would have the chance to be employed with uniforms and pay. It would keep a lot of the young hotheads occupied and out of trouble. Also give them some discipline."

"The parlay is over, then?" Molly asked.

Father Jutz nodded. He pulled a handkerchief from his coat pocket and wiped the meat grease from his mouth and hands. "That was delicious. I've got to get a nap. I'm exhausted." He pushed himself up from the square of canvas they were sitting on.

"You won't be returning to the Stronghold?"

"No, but Brooke said you'll be going back, this time with Louis Shangreau. Brooke said he was also sending about thirty of the peaceful Miniconjous to help persuade them." The old man's eyes crinkled in a tired grin. "General Brooke wants you and the friendlies to ride back there tomorrow."

"Oh, no," Coyle groaned, glancing at

Molly. "What does he think I can do?"

"Wants a non-partisan, responsible witness, I suppose. You and the half-blood, Shangreau, will carry the message that the dancers will be given full rations if they give up. Basically, Brooke is promising to live up to the government's Eighteen Seventy-Six agreement."

"I hope they believe that."

"Thad, I don't want you to go back there again," Molly said quietly after Father Jutz left.

Coyle shrugged. "It's damned hard and frustrating, but it's my job. I have to co-operate with the Army now that the military is officially in charge of the reservation. It's a cinch Brooke isn't going to send Royer."

"I just have a feeling you're pushing your luck," she said, not looking at him. "Call it a woman's intuition, if you will. Many of these people are very kind-hearted. But, as you know, when they're backed into a corner, many of them can turn hostile in a moment."

"I'm touched that you're so concerned about me."

"I have only two close friends on this reservation . . . and they're women. You and I have common interests." She turned to face him. "And besides. . . ." She let her voice trail off.

He swallowed hard, and forced himself to

answer. "Molly, I'm very fond of you, but we can't let this go too far. I'm still married."

"Doesn't sound like much of a marriage to me," she replied matter-of-factly. "I live for the here and now. We have no guarantees for tomorrow."

He wondered if he should tell her about the letters he and Emma had been exchanging. Ten months ago, more than four years after she'd left, he'd received a letter from her. It bore the postmark of Cairo, Illinois. His hands had shaken as he opened it, but the tone of the letter was friendly and chatty, giving no explanation for her actions. It was as if they'd just seen each other last week. As he had read it through tear-dimmed eyes, he had thought of his son and daughter who had spent most of their growing-up years without him. He puzzled once again over Emma's mental state. She was apparently one of those married women who was perfectly happy to live without her husband. Was there another man? Knowing what little he did of her, he seriously doubted it. External stability seemed to be what she instinctively sought.

He had immediately and joyfully answered the letter, bringing her up to date on the events of his life. After that, they'd corresponded on a regular basis like two old friends. For fear of driving her away again,

Coyle had kept his letters on a friendly, rather than an intimate, basis. Five months ago he'd been assigned to report on the ghost dance situation at the Pine Ridge Agency, and he'd written her four letters since he'd been here, being careful not to mention Molly Seeker. And now, he saw no need to mention the letters to Molly, either.

Molly rose, brushed off her skirt, and turned away. "I'll expect you for supper . . . if you're not afraid to be alone with me." She gave him a quick smile over her shoulder, then walked away without looking back.

The trip back to the Stronghold was made on agency horses. Tired as he was, Coyle was thankful for not having to bounce in a wagon and for the fact that the weather had moderated. The sun was shining when the party arrived, and they found a ghost dance in progress on the grassy plateau. The Lakota leaders who'd been left behind refused to interrupt the dance to hold a conference. Coyle was able to get a few hours of sleep inside one of the vacant tents.

It wasn't until the next afternoon that Kicking Bear and Short Bull condescended to meet with the party.

"The agent will forgive you, if you come in now," Louis Shangreau told them when he,

Coyle, and the Sioux leaders of both sides were gathered in the warm sunshine outside Kicking Bear's tent. "The agent will increase your rations. The only restriction is that you may not dance the ghost dance."

Short Bull stood in front of the seated Shangreau and Coyle, and his manner and tone told Coyle the substance of the reply before he even heard Shangreau's translation.

"If the great father would allow us to continue the dance, give us more rations, and stop taking away pieces of our reservation for white farmers, we would favor returning," Shangreau interpreted. "But we know that, if we return, the soldiers will put some of us in jail for stealing cattle and plundering houses. We are free now and have plenty of beef, and can dance all the time in obedience to the Messiah's command. You can go back to your agent and tell him that the Lakotas are not coming in."

When Shangreau finished, Short Bull gestured that he was finished and said something in Lakota. The crowd of people behind him began crowding back toward the flattened grass of the dance ground. Another ghost dance started in spite of Coyle's and the half-breed's protests that they had to continue the talks.

The two men and the thirty friendly

Miniconjous were ignored for two days and nights while the dance continued without let-up. Dozens of the frenzied dancers fell with exhaustion and visions. It seemed the longest two days Coyle had ever spent. He put in his time catching up on his sleep, and then examining the area of the plateau. The sentries watched him warily at first, but soon decided he was no threat. After observing the dancers for a time, he wandered off by himself to take a closer look at the perimeter of the plateau. He soon discovered why this place was called the Stronghold. It was very defensible by a small force. Steep, crumbling sides dropped away at least four hundred feet on every side. There was adequate firewood in the eroded ravines leading to the cliff edges and enough grass to last the cattle and horses until spring. By then, if their beliefs were realized, the Messiah would come, and they would have no further need of the Stronghold.

Coyle tugged his hat down against the chill gusts and looked out over the edge, following the dun-colored grass of the rolling South Dakota plain to where earth and sky joined on the horizon. In spite of the sometimes harsh climate, it was a wide-open, beautiful country. Over the centuries one people after another had dominated the land. Currently it was a race of whites from the East who were forcing out the Lakotas. He wondered who would be the next. Certainly his generation would not be around to see future conquests. No wonder most Indians could not grasp the concept of humans actually *owning* the earth. But in the here and now, the Lakota leaders were stalling, trying to delay the inevitable. It was typical of their negotiations. He was not discouraged. As definite as Short Bull's answer had been, Coyle knew there was no logic or certitude to their thought processes. Often white patience was the best tool. It would all be over soon, and would end in total surrender of the Lakotas. Coyle was impatient for the final result. As long as it was coming anyway, let it happen quickly.

The next day the conference finally resumed. This time the talk was short. What Coyle expected happened quickly. Two Strike rose to his feet and announced that he was taking his people to Pine Ridge. Not to be outdone, the medicine man chief, Crow Dog, then stood and said he was going to do the same.

Short Bull leaped up, shouting in English: "At such a time we should stick together like brothers! These agency men are lying. They will take you to the agency and put you in jail. Louis Shangreau and this white man, Coyle, are responsible for this. Kill them! Kill *them!*" His voice rose to a frenzied shout.

Fired by his passion, the crowd surged forward. Apparently afraid to shoot for fear of hitting friends, many of Short Bull's followers charged Shangreau and Coyle, swinging their rifles like clubs.

Instantly the crowd of friendly agency Indians surrounded the two men. In seconds a mêlée broke out, with rifle butts and stone war clubs thudding against heads and upraised arms. Then the crash of gunfire drowned every other sound.

Coyle crouched next to Shangreau as the fighting factions surged around them. Watching in all directions to protect himself, Coyle spotted Crow Dog who was taking no part in the brawl. The Indian leader pushed his way to the center of the club-swinging mob and sat down on the ground, pulling his blanket over his head.

The effect was almost magical. A few of the men noticed him and backed away. Then more Indians stopped shouting and swinging. Within the space of half a minute the bloody free-for-all subsided and stopped. Except for several Lakotas who lay moaning and bleeding on the ground, an eerie silence ensued as all eyes were on the huddled, blanket-covered figure. Shangreau and Coyle stood up to see what had happened. Between the shoulders of two friendly Miniconjous, Coyle saw Crow Dog fling off his blanket. The chief stood up and threw his arms wide. "Brothers!" he shouted. "Stop this! I cannot stand to see Lakota blood being shed by Lakotas." He paused and looked around him. The only sound was the wind and the harsh breathing of several combatants. "I am going now to the agency. You can kill me if you wish, but the great father's words are true. It is better to return than to stay here." With that he snatched up his blanket and strode away.

That ended the fighting. As Coyle and Shangreau went looking for their horses, the half-blood scout said in an undertone: "That was too damned close. I'm not complaining, mind you, but those were mighty strange words, coming from Crow Dog. A few years back he murdered Spotted Tail in one of these factional disputes."

"Maybe that's why he stopped this before they began killing each other," Coyle replied. "Matter of fact, I wouldn't be surprised if one or more of them weren't killed back there just now."

The two men were careful to stay together while the village stirred to life and made ready to depart. When they finally moved out, Coyle estimated about a thousand people were following Crow Dog and Two Strike. As those on foot and horseback filed across the narrow land bridge, Coyle looked back. He guessed Kicking Bear and Short Bull now retained the allegiance of only about two hundred of the Brulé and Oglala people who remained behind at the Stronghold.

The hold-outs were now in the minority, Coyle noted with satisfaction. Only the followers of Sitting Bull at Standing Rock, and those of Big Foot, still advocated the ghost dance religion. He was optimistic that, if steady pressure were to be kept up by the military and civilian authorities, the movement could be worn down and dissipated. It was probably the only way an open war might be avoided.

Facing forward in the saddle, Coyle felt better than he had for a long time. Even the cold wind in his face failed to irritate him.

Chapter Fifteen

December 18, 1890
Camp of Big Foot's Miniconjou band
South of the Cheyenne River

Tom Merritt, now using his old name, Swift Hawk, was apprehensive about the young hot bloods just outside Big Foot's tent. He had no idea how they would react to the news. Sitting Bull was dead, killed by agency police who were attempting to arrest him. Two of Sitting Bull's Hunkpapa warriors had arrived from Standing Rock this morning, one with a bullet in his leg. The story they told was somewhat sketchy, but apparently Agent James McLaughlin, a long-time foe of Sitting Bull, had sent a detachment of tribal police under Bull Head and Red Tomahawk to arrest Sitting Bull at his cabin. The agent feared the old chief and his followers would bolt the reservation without permission and join the ghost dancers at the Stronghold.

The arrest had been attempted just before dawn in a freezing rain three days ago. At first Sitting Bull had consented to go peacefully, but his seventeen-year old son ridiculed him for being weak, and the old bull balked. Harsh words were followed by pushing and shoving, and someone from the tribe fired a shot at the police. In the mêlée that followed, Sitting Bull was shot in the head. His son was killed, along with six policemen and several of the chief's defenders.

A company of soldiers from Fort Yates had arrived the next day. With artillery fire they drove off a group of the old bull's followers who were laying siege to the surviving tribal police holed up in the cabin. The fleeing Hunkpapas said that more of their refugee band would be arriving to seek help from Big Foot in the next day or two.

Swift Hawk could hear Talks With Horses and Yellow Bird outside, arguing with others about the best course to follow. Several of the young men possessed late-model Winchester rifles, and were adamant that something should be done to avenge Sitting Bull's death. But they couldn't decide how to retaliate, Swift Hawk realized as he strained to catch snatches of the excited talk. Some were for killing Agent McLaughlin who had sent the police after Sitting Bull. Others wanted to kill the first white man they saw, although no one proposed attacking the Army units that were within thirty miles of their present camp.

Swift Hawk sensed the frustration. After all, Sitting Bull had been killed by his own people who wore the blue coats and metal badges of the agency police. It seemed the Lakota people were turning inward and destroying themselves. Even Sitting Bull's old friend, Hump, had gone over to walk the white man's road.

Big Foot's daughter Gray Dove lifted the tent flap and entered. Without looking at Swift Hawk, she bent over her father with a bowl of some kind of meat, spooning the concoction into his mouth. The old man was propped up on one elbow, but was very weak. Age and the lack of proper food and shelter had brought on catarrh the week before. The alternating cold and mild weather had seen the congestion turn into what Swift Hawk suspected was pneumonia — a very dangerous illness from which he'd seen many white prospectors die.

"How do you feel, Father?" Gray Dove asked, setting the bowl aside and wiping his mouth.

"Better." He coughed with a deep, rattling sound.

He didn't sound better, but Swift Hawk knew the old man was fighting the sickness, trying to keep control of his band. Outside, the loud argument had faded. Either the young braves had stopped shouting at each other, or they had moved out of earshot. *I've lived too long in white society,* Swift Hawk thought. He'd forgotten how elemental his people were. The harshness of life and death were not disguised here. The Lakotas seemed almost child-like to him now. He felt he had to return to help Standing Elk, known to the whites as Big Foot, persuade his band of Miniconjous to make peace at all cost. No doubt the old ways were proud and glorious, but they were gone, never to return — in spite of the beliefs of the ghost dancers. Swift Hawk had come to help Big Foot convince the People of this. But now the old man was very sick and might not live long. Age and the elements had conspired to weaken and bring him down, like wolves harassing an old buffalo. If Big Foot died, Swift Hawk might as well return to Rapid City and his former way of life as Tom Merritt, freighter. The hard, cold stares and remarks from those of his own age, and younger, reminded him constantly that he was now an unwelcome outsider who had abandoned them years before. It had probably been a mistake to return here. Yet, he felt compelled to try, since these Lakotas were of his same flesh and spirit. As one who had made his own successful way in the white world, he felt qualified to teach others of his kind how to do the same. Those who did not adapt to change perished. It was true of all species. Those giant beasts whose bones were occasionally eroded out of the soft Badlands soil had died off centuries before. Perhaps they could not cope with change. On the other hand, the opportunistic coyote had learned to live with man, adapting its omnivorous habits from finding carrion and small game to raiding chicken houses.

Swift Hawk sighed, staring with unseeing eyes at Gray Dove, while his mind drifted to that December day nine years ago when Coyle had quit the freighting partnership and gone back to his wife. He and Thad Coyle had been business partners from 1876 until the end of 1881, and had fit together like a straight, fletched arrow to a well-strung bow. There were never any complaints or arguments, while each man pulled his weight and shared equally in the profits. Although of different races, they had been bound together by mutual respect between outcasts. After Coyle had left, Merritt had hired a succession of helpers, most of them half-breeds. For one reason or another, not one of them had stayed more than a few months. It was those early years of the Black Hills gold rush that had been the best for him. But there was no use pining for those good, gone days, any more than there was for Lakotas bewailing the loss of a free-roaming past.

He had to deal with the practicalities of the present. And just his being here was the strangest part of all. It had been while he was outfitting himself with a new suit of clothing in a Denver emporium two months ago that he'd been struck by something mystical, yet almost physical. He couldn't explain it then, and he couldn't explain it now. But, as he regarded himself in a full-length mirror with the salesman standing at his shoulder, a white-hot flash of guilt seemed to shake his whole body. Whose lean, dark face stared back at him above the white collar and black broadcloth? *Are you Swift Hawk?* he heard a silent voice ask, *the man who sold out your people for more than thirty pieces of Caucasian silver?* The sensation was so real, he'd looked quickly around for the source, but nobody else had been present. He'd begun to sweat, then to tremble, and finally had to take off the suit and leave the store.

From that day he'd felt no peace until he sold his freighting outfit and showed up at Big Foot's camp three weeks later with money to buy food and blankets. He begged the old man to allow him to return and to help with both money and persuasion. Big Foot welcomed him back as if he'd never left.

For the past five weeks, Swift Hawk had

been quietly urging the younger Lakotas to accept him as a brother and to listen to their older, wiser leaders. Although he had strong doubts about the imminent return of the Messiah Who would rescue only Indians, he had paid one of the older wives in the band to make him a ghost shirt from a soft piece of tanned elk hide he'd brought with him. He wore the shirt, now and then, to show silently his oneness with the believers. But, at the same time, he reminded them the original ghost dance religion taught love and kindness — not hatred and defiance. He patiently echoed Big Foot's words, urging his people to be practical — not to expect outside help from a savior who would be brought to earth by the gyrations of an hypnotic dance.

Gray Dove pulled the blanket up around her father's shoulders. "Rest now, and get your strength." She gave Swift Hawk an unfathomable look, then took the bowl and spoon, and left the tent.

Swift Hawk hunkered down and watched the old man for two or three minutes. The chief's eyes were closed, and he was lying back, breathing deeply, apparently asleep.

But then the chief opened his eyes and said: "Bring Talks With Horses and Yellow Bird and the others here. We have to talk."

Swift Hawk quickly went out and did as requested. Ten minutes later, six men were in the tent, Talks With Horses carrying his rifle.

The old man began with no preliminaries. "The half-blood scout from Colonel Sumner's camp told me that Bear Coat Miles expects us to join our kinsmen at the Stronghold," he said.

"Yes, yes," Talks With Horses said eagerly. "We should all go there. Then let the blue coats try to get us!"

Big Foot looked impatient at this outburst, then continued. "We are as yet many miles from the Stronghold. Since the Army thinks we go there, they will send the soldiers to ride quickly to stop us. Because they expect it, we must not go there."

There was a chorus of dissent from three of the warriors.

Big Foot held up his hand for silence, as he sat cross-legged on the ground, a blanket drawn about his shoulders. "We must keep them confused. They must not be sure of what we will do. Our brothers, the Oglalas, at Pine Ridge have offered me a hundred horses to come south and join them at the agency. But that is also a long way, and I am not feeling well. My friend, Colonel Sumner, who is watching us with two-hundred soldiers, wants us to go to the nearest agency at Cheyenne River."

"If we can reach the Stronghold, they cannot capture us," Yellow Bird said in a low voice. "You wished all of our people to dance the ghost dance and resist the whites. We can do that at the Stronghold."

Swift Hawk wondered if Yellow Bird's wild-eyed look was an indication of his mental state, or if he was just trying to enhance his stature as a medicine man.

"Even if we could reach there before the blue coats, they will wait many moons for us to starve up there. But it is not about the Stronghold that we must be concerned now." He paused and took several deep breaths. Swift Hawk thought the old man looked flushed, feverish.

"Our kinsmen, the Hunkpapas, have fled to us from Sitting Bull's camp and need our help. They are nearly naked and starving. We must not turn them away. I will tell Colonel Sumner this. If we cannot reach one of the agencies, we will return to our own camp on the Cheyenne River and remain there peacefully."

"The hair-mouth soldiers will not leave us alone until they have us locked up in their metal houses!" Talks With Horses spat bitterly. "The half-breed scout told me Colonel Sumner has orders from Bear Coat Miles to arrest the leaders of the Miniconjous and take us to jail at Fort Meade."

"Us? Are you a chief now also?" Big Foot asked sarcastically.

Talks With Horses turned aside and mumbled something to his nearest neighbor.

"What was that you said?" Big Foot asked sharply. The effort produced a wracking cough.

When the old man had regained his breath, Talks With Horses replied: "I said, since you gave up encouraging the ghost dance, you have become a weak old woman, afraid of the whites!"

Swift Hawk thought if the old man had had the strength, Talks With Horses would have died on the spot. As it was, Big Foot only glared at his accuser and said: "It was not always so. But to be a chief one must not only be brave, he must have the wisdom to know when to make peace."

"Peace?" Talks With Horses cried, emboldened. "You mean surrender!"

"One warrior does not go unarmed against a raging grizzly," Big Foot replied. "Such a grizzly is Bear Coat Miles. He has teeth and claws and strength and speed. No. The warrior knows he cannot win, so he feints and dodges and runs. He keeps the bear guessing. We will do the same. And our people will survive," he added, then paused to take several deep breaths. The men surrounding his pallet waited patiently for him to continue.

From years past, Swift Hawk had heard of the diplomatic skills of this man. He was well known within the tribe as a peacemaker and one who could settle disputes by compromise. It was a skill he put to good use in dealing with white politicians and soldiers who thought all Indians intellectually inferior because their culture was more primitive. Big Foot rarely made any flat statements, never drew a line in the dirt from which there was no retreat. Rather, he stalled, feinted, dodged, was ambiguous, gave ground only grudgingly, told the white treaty-makers one thing and his own followers something slightly different.

"The half-blood scout said that Colonel Sumner is only a few miles west of here. I will meet with him again. He is a good man, and we trust each other. His men will not harm us if we do nothing foolish." He looked pointedly at Talks With Horses who still held the Winchester. "Help me up. Hitch my horses. We will take my wagon to meet with Sumner now."

The men moved to obey. Even Talks With Horses and Yellow Bird seemed subdued by the calm insistence of this old man. Their instinctive respect for their elders won out.

Swift Hawk and Big Foot's daughter shared

Within the next several days, some forty of Sitting Bull's followers arrived in camp and were given succor. Much to Big Foot's chagrin, a few of them returned the favor by stealing some horses and departing in the night.

Meanwhile, the sick old chief and Swift Hawk, along with several others, urged the young hotheads of the Miniconjous to go to the nearest agency. Big Foot told them he had promised Sumner he would take his people east to the Cheyenne River Agency. With a glint in his rheumy eyes, the old man added that the real reason he'd agreed to Sumner's request was because December 22nd was ration day. "I did not tell Colonel Sumner we would *stay* there."

The next day John Dunn, a white rancher known as Red Beard to the Lakotas, rode into camp, along with half-breed interpreter, Felix Benoit. Dunn had been peddling butter and eggs at Sumner's camp, and the colonel requested that Dunn visit the Miniconjou camp to ask his friend, Big Foot, why he had not come to the Cheyenne River Agency as promised.

Big Foot replied smoothly that he was afraid to face the colonel until he had found the Hunkpapas who had come to him for help and then fled with the horses.

"Big Foot, you have been my friend for

the duties of driving the chief's wagon, while a dozen men rode as an armed escort. From previous visits during the past week, they knew the location of Col. Sumner's troops, approximately six miles to the west and south.

A north wind had kicked up, rattling sleet against the stiffened canvas that covered the wagon bows. Every few minutes, Swift Hawk glanced back to see the old man curled into a ball under the blankets in the wagon bed. There was little they could do to make him comfortable, as the bitter wind whistled and the bumps jolted them mercilessly.

About mid-afternoon, they came in sight of Sumner's camp on the banks of the partially frozen Cheyenne River and halted while the pickets sent word to the colonel. Ten minutes later Sumner was riding toward them with an escort of three men. He dismounted, and the tailgate of the wagon was lowered. Big Foot had pushed himself to a sitting position, his back leaning against the wagon box.

Then everyone else withdrew out of earshot to allow the two chiefs to talk privately. Their parlay lasted nearly thirty minutes and seemed to Swift Hawk to be very cordial. Near the end of their talk, Sumner motioned for one of his escort to approach. Apparently the man was a surgeon, Swift Hawk thought, as he watched the overcoated soldier examining Big Foot. He listened to the chief's chest and put a hand to the Indian's forehead. He spoke quietly to him. As he helped the old man wrap up once more in the blankets, the officer handed him a silver flask of something. The old man smiled and took two large swallows. He nodded and returned the flask. The soldier withdrew, and the chief and Col. Sumner spoke a few parting words before he and his escort mounted and rode back to their camp.

The Indians' horses, which had been watered while they waited, were now turned back for the return trip. The wind was in their faces, making the going slow. Gray Dove climbed into the back of the wagon and lay down next to her father, wrapping them both in the tattered blankets.

Swift Hawk drove the team, becoming silently more depressed by the weather and this whole miserable situation. He would have to wait until they arrived back in camp to find out what had transpired between the chief and Sumner. Swift Hawk knew Sumner and two companies of cavalry had been sent north by General Brooke at Pine Ridge to keep watch on Big Foot's band of Miniconjous, encouraging the old chief to lead his people into the nearest agency and camp. Giving up their guns was a matter that had not yet come up.

Even Hump, that fierce old warrior who'd helped defeat Custer and the 7th, was now encouraging peace. There had been much maneuvering back and forth these past two weeks with various military units and Indian bands. Because of the distances, communication among all of them was sadly lagging. News and messages had to travel by mounted couriers.

Swift Hawk suspected Col. Sumner had been, or would be, ordered to arrest Big Foot to eliminate his influence with his people. But the old chief and Sumner were friends who personally liked and respected each other. However, this did not change the fact of their official relationship, unless the colonel went out on a limb and ignored the arrest order. Swift Hawk could only wait and see. In the meantime, he would do all he could to influence the band give up and obey Col. Sumner and report to the Cheyenne River Agency to the east.

If the Messiah did not actually appear as pected in the spring, Swift Hawk intended encourage some of the younger Lakota to go off the reservation as individual make new lives for themselves. Than Carlisle and the agency schools, most could now speak, read, and write J Since that barrier was broken, the oth lems of race could somehow be deal

several years," Dunn told the old chief in fluent Lakota, as Swift Hawk and several others stood listening. "Because you are my friend, I will tell you something. You must take your people and go south quickly to the Pine Ridge Agency. I overheard Colonel Sumner say he has orders to come here in the night and capture you. General Bear Coat Miles has ordered Sumner to take your people to Fort Meade, and then to a prison on an island in the sea."

"Why are you telling me this?" Big Foot asked. "If the Army attempts to arrest us, I will fight and die right here on my own land. There is no need to flee south."

"I am warning you because we are friends," Dunn said. "And, besides, I have many cattle on the Belle Fourche River, near here. I would stand to lose them in a bloody war. Don't let Colonel Sumner know that I have revealed Army secrets to you."

Swift Hawk had been among many white men and instinctively distrusted this red-bearded Dunn. But, as soon as Dunn and the half-breed departed, a great stir and panic arose in camp, with Talks With Horses, Yellow Bird, and others strongly urging Big Foot to go south to Pine Ridge and join the Oglalas who had offered him a hundred horses to join them. "Colonel Sumner cannot arrest so many, once we join our brothers," Talks With

Horses said. "If you won't go to the Strong-hold, let us at least go to Pine Ridge!"

Feeling betrayed by Sumner, Big Foot finally agreed. Preparations began just after dark, about five o'clock. Evacuation of the camp proceeded in silence, but with a sense of urgency. Several hundred men, women, and children hurried to pile tent poles, pots and pans, and blankets into the wagons. As they hitched their teams, a bitter wind whipped manes and tails of the horses, tugging at the tight canvas wagon covers.

Swift Hawk stuffed his few belongings into a canvas bag, wondering what he would do if an armed clash came. A fight wasn't likely, he reasoned, yet he couldn't dismiss the possibility. He was armed with a Smith & Wesson .44 Russian model, but would he side with his own people in a do-or-die struggle? If not, why had he bothered to come back to the reservation? It was to help prevent just such a conflict, he thought. He considered himself a peacemaker. But if pushed too far. . . .

He shoved the thought from his mind. If it came to a showdown, he knew what he would do. Blood was a stronger tie than life style. He climbed to the seat of Big Foot's wagon and took up the reins as the Miniconjou people rolled out on their long, evasive journey south toward the Badlands.

Chapter Sixteen

"I'll be damned! It *is* Comanche!" Coyle exclaimed, walking toward the gelding that was being held by a sergeant of the 7th cavalry. "Never thought I'd see that old war horse again."

The bay was heavier than Coyle remembered, and his winter coat was grayer, but the scars were unmistakable, along with the short white sock on the left hind fetlock and the white star on the forehead.

"Captain Keogh's horse," the sergeant said, eyeing Coyle warily.

"I know."

"He is not to ride. We brought him along only for show. He is for the younger men a symbol of old times in the regiment," the man said in careful English, heavily accented by German.

"What's your name, Sergeant?"

"Gustave Korn," the man replied. "I am

the caretaker of this fine animal."

"Where are you from?"

"Fort Riley."

"I know that's where the Seventh is stationed. But where are *you* from?"

"Switzerland is my country. But I am American now," he responded proudly, squaring his shoulders as he held the reins of Comanche. Judging by the grizzled walrus mustache and the stripes on his sleeves, Coyle guessed this man to be one of the numerous immigrants who'd joined the United States military, found a home, and made it a career.

Glancing again at the horse, Coyle reflected that many of the raw recruits from big city slums who'd never seen an Indian until now probably needed some living connection with the tradition of Custer's old regiment.

"Pride is what it's all about," Coyle remarked, stroking Comanche. "Good luck, Sergeant," he said, turning away. He stopped short when he saw Molly Seeker, standing nearby.

"Renewing old acquaintances?" she asked, pulling the shawl closer around her head and averting her face from the stinging grit on the gusting wind.

"Something like that," Coyle replied absently, bittersweet memories crowding his mind. The last time he'd seen this horse was that December day in 1881 at Fort Meade when he and Emma had been unexpectedly and joyfully reunited. His stomach knotted at the thought of the ups and downs, the triumphs and tragedies of his life since he'd been court-martialed in 1876.

"Want to talk about it?" Molly asked as she took his arm, and they walked toward the agency offices.

He felt her eyes searching his face, and wondered how much of what he felt was showing. He'd never been good at hiding his feelings. And this woman was unusually perceptive. He shook his head. "Not just now." He gave her hand a squeeze to let her know that she was not the cause of his anguish. He held the door for her as they entered the agency offices. No need to go into his recent correspondence with Emma. If these letters hadn't led to anything further in ten months, he doubted that they ever would. It was a strange relationship for a husband and wife, he reflected, staring out the window at the bleak, deserted street.

Coming out of his reverie, Coyle turned away from the office window. The clacking of Molly's typewriter breached his consciousness. A hard gust of wind rattled the front door, and Coyle could feel the cold air flowing around his booted legs. He turned toward the stove and reached for the steaming coffee pot.

"I'm going over to the telegraph office," Agent Daniel Royer said, as he abruptly came out of his office and removed the dead stub of a cigar from his mouth. He reached for his overcoat and muffler. "Can't depend on them to run any messages over here as soon as they come in."

Coyle poured himself a cup of strong coffee and looked inquisitively at the agent over the rim of the heavy china mug.

"Should have heard something from the military by now. They're supposed to keep me apprised of what's going on. And where's that damned police lieutenant of mine . . . Thunder Bear? It's like I wasn't even the agent here." He clapped his derby on his head and went out the door, letting in a rush of cold air with the swirling snowflakes.

If you wanted to run this operation, you shouldn't have called in the Army, Coyle thought, watching the door slam behind him.

Christmas had come and gone, and still the ghost dance situation dragged on. Coyle thought the movement of the troops, the civilians, the agency police, agency Indians, and the various ghost dance bands was like some slow, giant chess game. The board was so large and spread out that no one knew exactly what moves the others had made. For anyone used to quick, decisive action, it was very frustrating. And Royer, his fears allayed by the presence of the soldiers, still wanted to remain on the front line of spectators, fearful of his own reputation. He didn't want to be shoved aside and forgotten. Kicking Bear, Short Bull, and about three hundred of their ardent ghost dance followers still held out at the Stronghold. But where was Big Foot and his people? Sick as the old man reportedly was, his band had managed to elude the cavalry. If they were headed for the Stronghold, surely they would have arrived there by now.

A ratcheting noise intruded on his thoughts as Molly rolled another sheet of paper into her typewriting machine. She looked curiously at him. "I can give you something to do, if you're bored," she said. "I'd be going out of my mind since the school shut down, if it weren't for this job."

"I'm never bored when I'm around you," he parried, grinning at her. He strode to the window again and looked out. His stomach grumbled, and he realized he'd consumed nothing today but coffee.

A rider came galloping down the dirt street. Coyle recognized Thunder Bear as he materialized out of the whirling snowflakes, pulled up, and dismounted. The door was flung open and the police lieutenant looked quickly around the office.

"Where is Royer?"

"At the telegraph office. I'm acting for him," Coyle replied.

"Big Foot's band is camped on Wounded Knee Creek, east of here."

"Last I heard they were headed for the Stronghold," Coyle said.

Thunder Bear nodded.

"Are they coming in to the agency to surrender? Did they change their minds about joining the ghost dancers?"

Molly had stopped typing, and the only sound was the fire settling in the stove and the wind rattling the wooden shutters.

"Big Foot is an old fox. I do not know what is in his mind. I have just ridden from his camp, and know that he is very sick. Maybe he cannot live to reach the Stronghold."

"So, now there are only about three hundred ghost dancers still at the Stronghold," Coyle commented.

"The agency chiefs here tell me Short Bull and Kicking Bear have agreed to surrender. They will lead their followers here to Pine Ridge on December Twenty-Ninth. They have sent word to Big Foot to time his travel so he will come in here the same day."

Coyle was startled. How had he missed this

news? The ghost dance hold-outs had sent messengers to the agency and to Big Foot without the whites knowing anything about it.

"Do the soldiers know where Big Foot is?" Coyle asked.

"Yes. Major Whitside's soldiers rode out to meet Big Foot and his people on Porcupine Creek. Then they all rode into camp on Wounded Knee Creek."

"What do they plan to do?" Coyle asked.

The police lieutenant shrugged, his black eyes revealing nothing of his feelings. If he had any personal opinions about the situation, he was not divulging them.

"Royer might want to talk to you," Coyle said as an afterthought. "He's waiting for messages over the telegraph wire."

The Indian departed without a word.

"I think there's more going on here than we know," Coyle said to Molly. "Do you feel like taking a ride over to Wounded Knee Creek?"

"That's nearly twenty miles. It's awfully cold and windy outside," she replied dubiously.

"What do you expect in South Dakota this time of year?"

"You think there's going to be a confrontation of some kind?" she asked.

"I don't know, but I have a strange feeling

about this." He paced to the window and looked out toward the military encampment south of town where an unusual amount of activity was taking place. He watched closely for a couple of minutes. Horses were being saddled, but tents were not being struck.

"The cavalry is stirring," he said, turning back to her. "I'd bet Colonel Forsyth is taking the Seventh over to Wounded Knee."

"Why?" She looked up.

"Adding the force of numbers to Whitside's cavalry just to make sure nothing spooks Big Foot's band again before they get here to the agency. General Miles would have their hide if Big Foot gets away a second time." He smiled wryly. "I think the Army would call this providing an escort."

"I'll go with you. Wait until I finish typing this letter."

"No. We should leave now."

She glanced up sharply at his tone, then silently touched the release, slipped the paper from the machine, and laid it on the desk. "Hand me my coat."

Chapter Seventeen

December 29, 1890
Wounded Knee Creek

Thad Coyle took a deep breath as he stepped into the sunshine.

"What a lovely morning!" Molly exclaimed, reflecting his own thought. Their breath was steam in the chill air, but the slanting rays were giving promise of a rapid warm-up. A spring-like day was on the way. An hour earlier, Coyle had vaguely heard — and ignored — the familiar staccato notes of a bugle sounding reveille.

They'd arrived at Wounded Knee in her buggy just after dark the previous evening. Even though the moonlit night wasn't below freezing and they could have camped out, Coyle had used his position as Special Indian Agent to secure shelter. They'd slept, fully dressed, on the floor of the log post office — she under his buffalo coat and he under a smelly horse blanket. At least, it was a roof and a floor. Louis Mousseau, a French mixed-blood who operated this combination post office and store, had also provided overnight shelter to three reporters. About eight-thirty, just before they'd bedded down, Coyle had stepped outside to investigate the soft thunder of hundreds of approaching hoofs. Four troops of the 7th cavalry from Pine Ridge were riding in, led by Col. James Forsyth.

In spite of the accommodations, he'd slept tolerably well. Molly looked a little rumpled this morning, but she was game. He couldn't picture Emma roughing it like this. But then, Emma would not have been teaching school on an Indian reservation, either.

They stood outside the post office, looking three hundred yards south where the sun was reflecting from orderly rows of white canvas. Just beyond the Army camp, the cone-shaped Indian teepees were grouped. Smoke from dozens of cooking fires rose straight up in the windless air as both soldiers and Indians set about their breakfasts. Squinting, Coyle could make out the blue uniforms of several hundred troops. "Let's take a walk," he suggested.

Molly fell in beside him as they made their way south among the Army tents. Aromas of woodsmoke and frying bacon filled the morning air, as men squatted at fires or sat cross-legged on ground cloths, eating.

They wandered among the tents, angling

away from the Indian camp, until Coyle spotted the guidon of the 7th cavalry hanging limply from a staff. Nearby sat the 7th cavalry farrier, Sgt. Gustave Korn, eating alone.

"Ah, Sergeant Korn, good morning."

The soldier looked up from dunking a piece of hardtack in his coffee cup. Coyle thought the long face and huge, drooping mustaches gave the man a Bassett-hound look.

"Good morning, Mister Coyle."

"You wouldn't have a little of that bacon and bread you could spare for a couple of hungry travelers, now, would you?"

The sergeant glanced at Molly, then gestured broadly at the pan near the fire. "Help yourself," he said in his heavy German dialect with no change of expression. "We have plenty. We are even feeding the prisoners."

"Prisoners?" Coyle asked, draping a thick strip of greasy bacon over a piece of hardtack and handing it to Molly.

"Indians," Korn answered.

A good gesture, Coyle thought with satisfaction. One of the best ways to placate these people was to keep their stomachs full, with promise of more to come. Years of Lakota discontent could have been prevented if the government had lived up to its treaty obligations of providing adequate food. But a stingy Congress, plus thievery of corrupt agents, had

241

sabotaged these agreements.

Korn handed over two tin cups, and Coyle poured coffee for Molly and himself. They had not eaten since noon yesterday, and the food was most welcome. They ate their fill, softening the nearly inedible hardtack in the strong coffee.

"I see you brought Comanche along," Coyle remarked, noting that the gelding was tethered near Korn's tent instead of with the other cavalry mounts.

"The horse goes where we go," the sergeant replied.

The old horse raised his head and pricked his ears forward as if he knew they were talking about him.

Coyle nodded. If the aging war horse was intended to provide inspiration for green troops, it made sense to bring him into the field with them. *But they wouldn't need much inspiration this day,* Coyle thought, sipping the steaming brew. This was strictly escort duty. From what he could see, the Army had the Lakota encampment completely surrounded and had even positioned several wheeled Hotchkiss guns on a level rise of ground to the west of where he stood in the cavalry camp.

During his years in the Army and the Indian Bureau, Coyle had learned to trust his instincts. Being right most of the time was what had gotten him successive promotions. But it looked as if his premonition of trouble had been wrong this time. Why had he dragged Molly along for this? He enjoyed her company, true enough. Yet it was more than that. Perhaps he realized the final capitulation of the Lakotas would take place here. Never again would there be war between these native people and the dominant whites. This was likely the last scene, and he wanted to be here to observe it.

The three reporters also quartered in Mousseau's store had sensed the historic significance as well. On the stroll from the post office, Coyle had seen Charles Allen of the Chadron *Democrat* and Bill Kelly of the *Nebraska State Journal* conversing. He'd even spotted his old nemesis, Thomas Carson of the *Omaha Bee*. Coyle had quickly turned away to keep from being noticed, but not before he saw that Carson's wide-brimmed hat concealed most of the smaller bandage he was now wearing around his head. The man was like a burr Coyle couldn't get rid of.

Coyle tossed the dregs of his coffee onto the ground and looked around. A sense of calm pervaded the whole area. There would be no trouble. From what he could see, the soldiers outnumbered the Sioux at least four to one. And probably two-thirds of the Sioux were women and children. True, if only half of Big Foot's braves carried Winchester repeaters, they would have superior firepower against the single-shot Springfields of the soldiers.

He shook his head to clear it of such thoughts. He was thinking like a military man again. Old habits die hard.

"Thanks, Sergeant Korn," Coyle said.

The old non-com nodded as Coyle and Molly dropped their cups into a nearby bucket of water and moved away, stepping around the guy ropes and tent pegs.

Between the cavalry and the Indians, three large Sibley tents stood apart from the others, with sentries posted nearby. On inquiry, Coyle discovered the middle tent was for Big Foot. A smoking stovepipe protruded through the canvas roof.

"The assistant surgeon is with him," the private on guard duty said. "The old man is pretty sick."

The tent on the east side was for Indians who had no shelter of their own, the guard said. And the one on the west was for the interpreters. A council ground stretched south of the big tents. Beyond this open space was the Indian camp.

As Coyle and Molly skirted the Indian camp, he noted the women chatting and singing softly as they loaded their wagons, preparing for the last leg of the journey in to Pine Ridge. Children were laughing and running among the lodges.

Some of the men stood in groups of two and three, talking and smoking. A few were still eating breakfast. Coyle took Molly's hand and led her up the sloping side of the flat-topped hill. The barrels of four Hotchkiss guns protruded outward from the crest of the rise.

"I never saw any guns like this," Molly said to a soldier who wore the red chevrons of an artillery sergeant.

"Best weapon ever developed for the field," the soldier replied proudly, rubbing a hand over the polished brass of the slim, tapered barrel.

"Seems rather small for a cannon," Molly remarked.

"Don't let the size fool you, ma'am. The shell may be only a little over three inches in diameter, but it weighs two and a half pounds. The Indians say it shoots twice because it explodes on impact. It's a devastating projectile for its size."

Coyle felt her give a little shudder as she let go of his hand. Before Coyle could say anything, the clear notes of Officers' Call split the morning air.

Coyle recognized Col. James Forsyth, resplendent in his blue uniform, pacing toward them. "As long as you're here, Mister Coyle, you might as well join us," Forsyth said. Then he touched his hat brim to Molly. "Miss Seeker."

Coyle knew Forsyth as a courteous, gallant officer who had the respect of his men. He even looked the part of a dashing cavalry officer — black hair, shot through with gray at the temples, black mustache, clear blue eyes, calm demeanor. From all accounts, Forsyth had not seen any hostile action against the Indians, but he was experienced in every other facet of military life.

In less than five minutes all the company commanders were assembled near Col. Forsyth, twenty yards behind the guns. Coyle and Molly stood to one side.

"Gentlemen," Forsyth began, "I have orders from General Brooke to disarm these Indians before we take them to Pine Ridge. The general was most emphatic that we must not allow any of them to escape." He paused. "I have a plan to disarm them quickly and efficiently. The Indian men and older boys are to be assembled near Big Foot's tent in the open area between the Indians and the cavalry camp. They will be kept in a compact group and surrounded by troops at all times. This should discourage any ideas of resistance."

"They aren't going to like giving up those Winchesters," Capt. Wallace remarked. "In most instances they've parted with a lot of their other belongings to buy them. They're mighty proud of those new repeaters."

"Might as well emasculate them," Capt. Varnum agreed. "A good rifle is a symbol of an Indian's manhood."

"Can't be helped," Forsyth said. "It's too dangerous to allow those guns to stay in their hands. Now . . . Captain Varnum, your B troop will form a line on foot about two hundred feet long along the northwest side of the council area. Place the men about a four feet apart." He pointed. "Captain Wallace, you'll do the same along the southwest side, forming a right angle with B troop. Forty men of A and I troops will form an east-west line between the cavalry tents and the foot of this hill to protect the artillery. The rest . . . about seventy-five men . . . will form a loose line around the south and west of the Indian village and well back away from it. Got that?"

The officers nodded.

"Captain Edgerly, take your G troop and establish a one-hundred-yard line well back to the southwest of the council area. Lieutenant Sickel, your mounted men will be on this low hill just west of us. Lieutenant Taylor, your Oglala scouts will form an east-west line two hundred yards long south of this ravine. And, finally, Captains Jackson and Godfrey, your C and D troops will stand in reserve, south of the Indian scouts."

"Sir," Capt. Wallace said in his soft South Carolina accent, "most of my men are raw recruits from big city slums. Some of 'em have barely learned to ride a horse. You think they should be so close to the Lakotas?"

"They have to get experience sometime, Captain," Forsyth replied shortly. "I don't want any inexperienced horsemen with nervous mounts. That's why I'm deploying your men on foot." He looked at their expectant faces. "If there's nothing else, let's get to it. The sooner we have this done, the better." He turned. "Bugler, sound Assembly."

The company commanders separated to relay their orders as the bugler moistened his lips. Non-coms barked commands; soldiers scrambled to finish eating as they grabbed for their Springfields.

"Wells!" Col. Forsyth called the half-breed interpreter, Phillip Wells, to him. "Tell the Indian men to assemble at Big Foot's tent for a council."

Wells nodded, and trotted down the hill while Assembly blared out in the still air.

Coyle watched and listened, saying nothing. His own past experience in deploying troops caused him to wonder at Forsyth's tactics. Would the Indians feel too tightly hemmed in? Would it cause them to panic and bolt? He and Molly strolled back to the gun battery and greeted Harry Hawthorne, a young lieutenant he'd recently met. The three of them looked out over the lower ground where the soldiers were forming perimeter lines.

Coyle could hear the camp crier, Indian Hand, singing out his message as he trotted among the lodges.

"Isn't that a rather strange formation of troops in case there's any trouble?" Coyle wondered aloud. "If a fight did break out, they wouldn't be able to shoot at the Indians without also shooting at each other."

Lt. Hawthorne laughed lightly. "Colonel Forsyth knows there's no possibility of trouble. Big Foot wants to go to the agency, and we're a guard of honor to escort him."

"Damnedest deployment I ever saw," Coyle whispered to Molly. "Makes me nervous, and I'm not even in charge of this operation."

The soldiers came up in line about three paces apart, casually resting their rifle butts on the ground. They formed a human fence between the council circle and the Indian camp to the south. Similar lines were formed on the other three sides of the council ground. Coyle's instincts told them the soldiers were pressed uncomfortably close to the Indians, but he said nothing.

Coyle slipped his watch from his vest pocket and popped open the case. It was eight-fifteen. By nine, this operation should be over, and they'd all be moving toward Pine Ridge. It couldn't happen too soon to suit him. He automatically wound the watch stem, then closed the case, and slid it back into his vest. He and Molly walked halfway down the sloping side of the flat hill below the guns where they could still see and hear the speech above the heads of the troops.

The sun was well above the horizon now, warming him through his gray corduroy jacket. He'd left the buffalo coat behind at the post office. Most of the Lakota men and boys had gathered, and interpreter John Shangreau seated them in a rough semicircle just to the south of Big Foot's tent. Forsyth was there to greet them, along with Major Whitside. The colonel calmly told the Lakota men that they were now safe. The soldiers were their friends, he assured them, pausing between each sentence or two for Shangreau to translate. Forsyth told them their rations had been increased so none of them would have to go hungry again. "However," the colonel went on, "there has recently been much trouble. We've had no fighting, but there has been great danger of it." He paused as Shangreau repeated his words in Lakota. "Therefore, to prevent some accidental fight, we must ask you to give us your guns."

As soon as Shagreau translated, the Indians stirred. A murmuring swept through the group like a sudden wind through prairie grass. Clearly this was not what they wanted to hear. A few of the men stood up. The charged atmosphere reminded Coyle of a herd of wild cattle, suddenly spooked and ready to stampede.

Forsyth stopped talking to let the Indians talk among themselves. In a few moments they told Shangreau they'd selected two of their number to confer with Big Foot.

Coyle let go of Molly's hand. "I'm going to Big Foot's tent with Shangreau," he whispered.

"What?" She looked her alarm at him.

"Don't worry. Most of these Indians know me. They won't be nervous because I'm not wearing a uniform." He slipped through the line of troopers and arrived at the white tent just as Shangreau lifted the flap to follow the two Lakotas inside. The stifling heat of the oil-burning stove struck Coyle immediately. He moved to one side along the wall and took in the scene. The chief lay on a pallet, a blanket wrapped outside the old gray overcoat. A scarf bound his head and was tied under the chin. In spite of the heat from the stove, the old man was visibly shivering. Big Foot's rheumy eyes were open, and a young woman — probably his daughter — crouched near him. An Army surgeon, Dr. Hoff, moved back from his patient as the two Indians squatted near the old man.

Coyle's encompassing gaze was suddenly arrested by another person in the tent. It was an Indian who was talking quietly to Big Foot's daughter. There was something familiar about him — the slender build, the hair pulled back in a ponytail. Coyle's eyes adjusted to the dimly lit interior, and he focused on this Indian who was dressed in a painted deerskin ghost shirt and ragged canvas pants. The man's eyes were older and there were lines around the mouth, but the face was unmistakable. It was Tom Merritt, his former freighting partner from years ago.

"Tom!" he blurted out before he could catch himself.

Merritt flashed him a warning glance, and Coyle looked away and hunkered down beside the tent wall. Yet his mind was in a whirl. What was his old, chain-smoking business partner doing here? And dressed in a ghost shirt at that?

252

The two Lakota men were already in conference with Big Foot. Shangreau was listening and suddenly broke in, shaking his head. "No, no. Don't give up only your old guns. Give up *all* of them." Big Foot turned his eyes on the interpreter who spoke in English. "These guns can easily be replaced," Shangreau went on. "But if you lose a man, you cannot replace him."

Big Foot did not change expression. "No!" His voice was surprisingly strong. "We will keep our good guns."

The delegation of two Indian men silently got up and ducked back under the tent flap into the sunshine outside. Coyle and Shangreau followed. The interpreter did not speak to the two officers. Whitside and Forsyth counted off twenty Indians and sent them into the camp to bring back all the guns.

The Indian men returned shortly with only two old, broken rifles. One was a muzzle-loader, the split stock wired together.

"What's this?" Major Whitside snapped, eyeing the battered weapons. "Looks like these have been used as toys for the children. I know you have plenty of guns . . . good ones. I saw them when I met you yesterday on Porcupine Creek."

"These are only guns in camp," one of the stone-faced Indians replied.

Whitside and Forsyth looked at each other. It was plain to Coyle they would have to call this bluff. "Let's bring Big Foot outside and make him order these men to surrender their guns," the major suggested.

Forsyth nodded, and directed four soldiers to bring out the chief. Dr. Hoff accompanied Big Foot as the old man was laid on a pallet, propped up on a rolled blanket in front of his tent.

"Tell him to make his people co-operate," Forsyth said to Phillip Wells who was standing nearby. Wells translated.

Big Foot replied, blinking up into the morning sun.

"He says they have no guns," Wells relayed. "He says the soldiers at Cheyenne River took them all away and burned them."

"Tell Big Foot that yesterday at the time of his surrender his men were well armed," Forsyth said. His voice was no longer smooth and conciliatory. "He is trying to deceive me."

Wells delivered the message in Lakota. Big Foot did not reply immediately as a fit of coughing racked his shivering frame. Coyle would have been inclined to feel sorry for the old warrior chief had he not known what a reputation Big Foot had for being a wily negotiator. Even though the chief was probably suffering from pneumonia, Coyle still felt the chief was using this cough to stall for time.

Coyle looked at the group of white men standing nearby. In addition to the soldiers, he saw two reporters — Charles Allen of the Chadron *Democrat* and Thomas Carson. The two men were talking to Father Craft, a young Catholic priest who assisted old Father Jutz at the mission. Coyle thought the black cassock stood out among the blue uniforms and the colorful blankets.

Big Foot stopped coughing and wiped his mouth. With the same pained expression as before, he repeated that he had given all his guns to the soldiers at the Cheyenne River Agency. "They burned all our weapons," Wells finished translating.

Whitside and Forsyth held a quick, quiet conference, which Coyle couldn't hear. "Captain Wallace and Lieutenant Mann, take fifteen men and John Shangreau to the east end of the camp. Search every tent. Only officers will enter the tents. This will be a very ticklish operation," Forsyth cautioned them, "so use the utmost tact. Captain Varnum and Lieutenant Garlington, take a detail along with Phillip Wells to the northwest end and do the same. Work your way back to this spot. I want every gun in this camp found and brought here."

The officers saluted, and selected their men. While the blanketed Indians looked on, the two squads started off on their search.

Even from a distance, Coyle could see that some of the enlisted men, ordered to search the outside areas, were going to extremes. They unloaded wagons and dumped over travois, scattering everything on the ground. They confiscated axes, butcher knives, war clubs, even quilling awls — anything that could possibly be considered a weapon. Coyle could not read any reaction on the faces of the onlooking Indians but knew that hate must be boiling in their hearts.

Coyle glanced back up the hill where he'd left Molly. She had moved down a little closer, but still stood high enough on the slope to see over the heads of the soldiers in front of her.

The women, who still sat among the lodges, had to be searched as well. Several times Coyle saw the men lift an Indian woman gently off a bundle to reveal a shiny Winchester under the voluminous folds of her skirt or under her blankets. The congenial Captain Wallace helped defuse what might have been a very tense operation by talking and joking with the women, through the interpreter, and playing with the children. Even though the soldiers rummaged roughly through the Indians' belongings, they were very gentle and respectful toward the women who would not voluntarily move.

"Gaw damn! Here's another new Winchester under this fat mama!" an enlisted man exclaimed as they lifted a corpulent Indian matron from a blanket and set her down a few feet away.

"Keep quiet, you men!" Lt. Mann ordered. "Just do your job and keep your mouths shut."

While the search progressed, an Indian whom Wells called Yellow Bird was dancing around the group, chanting something in Lakota. Now and then he paused, scooped up a handful of dirt, and tossed it into the air in the direction of the troops.

"What's he saying?" Forsyth demanded of Wells.

"He's making trouble," Wells said. "He's telling them to be strong and not be afraid of soldiers' bullets because the ghost shirts will cause the bullets to fly off over the prairie like the dust he's throwing in the air."

Forsyth and Wells walked over to Yellow Bird and told him to sit down and be quiet. Yellow Bird acted as if he didn't hear them. Yet, when he got to the other side of the circle, he squatted down and stopped chanting. But Coyle could see that Yellow Bird's gyrations and incantations had stirred up the stolid group of Indian men. They began to shift and mutter among themselves, their black eyes glaring at the line of soldiers who stood several yards away, holding their loaded Springfields.

The thorough search lasted until nearly nine-thirty, and the men returned to the council area with a large pile of hatchets, knives, and awls. But they had only thirty-eight rifles, many of which were old muskets and unusable.

"I know there are a lot more new rifles in this camp," Major Whitside muttered quietly. "I saw more than this yesterday."

"Well, if they're not in the lodges or the wagons and the women aren't hiding them, there's only one place left to look," Forsyth said. "The men are carrying them under their blankets." He turned to Wells. "Tell the men to come forward two at a time for inspection. They will pass between Captain Varnum and Major Whitside."

Phillip Wells translated, but the younger men returned only black looks and did not move.

Coyle's mouth was dry. This was the most dangerous part of the search. He wiped his sweating palms on his pants legs.

Finally about twenty of the older men got

up and came forward, each man dropping his blanket. No rifles were found, and they were shunted off to one side. Three of the younger men then stepped up. Two of them had rifles, which were confiscated.

"Now we're getting somewhere," Major Whitside said.

One of the younger bucks snatched up his blanket from the ground and stalked away angrily.

"Should we take the belts as well as the ammunition?" Capt. Varnum asked.

"No. Let them keep the belts," Whitside replied, dumping a handful of cartridges into the hat his first sergeant was holding. "Go find a grain bag to hold these shells," Varnum instructed another soldier.

Yellow Bird had started his harangue again, and the young men were becoming more agitated, moving around.

"Tell Big Foot to make them calm down," Forsyth said.

Wells translated, and the old chief barked something in Lakota. But his voice was too weak to be heard above the commotion.

"Who is that Indian?" Forsyth demanded, pointing at a young man who was strutting around, shouting and holding a rifle over his head with both hands.

"He is called Black Coyote," Wells replied.

"He is saying that he gave much money for his rifle and no one is going to get it unless they pay him for it." Wells paused. "Black Coyote is a little strange," he added, pointing at his own head.

"Disarm that man," Forsyth said.

A sergeant and a private quickly moved up behind Black Coyote and grabbed him. They forced his arms down, but the barrel of the weapon still pointed upward at an angle. The three men struggled for the Winchester. The hammer fell, and the gun fired, the blast slamming against Coyle's eardrums.

Out of the corner of his eye, Coyle saw Yellow Bird throw a handful of dirt into the air. As if the two simultaneous events were a signal, five or six young men threw off their blankets and brought up their hidden rifles, aiming them at the men of nearby K troop.

Chapter Eighteen

December 29, 1890
Wounded Knee Creek

"Look out! They're going to fire!" Lt. Robinson cried, swinging his horse out of the way. The first Indian volley smashed the air with a deafening blast.

"God! They've broken!" Capt. Varnum shouted.

"Fire! Fire on them!" Lt. Mann yelled. His voice was all but drowned in the stunning crash of answering shots from the soldiers' Springfields. A cloud of white smoke billowed into the windless air, obscuring everything. Coyle hit the ground, his ears filled with continuous volleys of gunfire like the loud ripping of canvas.

His first thought was of Molly. She was sensible enough to dive for the nearest cover. Oblivious to the deadly hail around him, Coyle rose to a crouch, yanked his Remington, then sprinted toward the surrounding line of soldiers. He had to get to her. Brass buttons glinting through the smoke and red jets of muzzle flashes were all he could see of the blurred figures of soldiers.

Right in front of him, an Indian with a knife lunged at Phillip Wells. Wells raised his Marlin with both hands to fend off the attack and deflected the blow, but the descending knife sliced off the end of his nose. Wells fired the rifle from the hip and cut down his attacker. Spurting blood, Wells staggered away, his nose dangling over his mouth by a piece of gristle.

Bullets were humming, and bodies falling in the murk. Coyle knew the Indian bullets that missed their mark were ripping into their own lodges beyond, while the soldiers' stray bullets were flying toward their comrades across the council ground. All was chaos. A few feet away, Lt. Garlington fell, grabbing his elbow. A bullet knocked the pipe from Capt. Varnum's mouth. Dr. Hoff scrambled for cover as lead messengers tugged at his clothing. Hand-to-hand fights broke out, and two grappling bodies slammed against Coyle, knocking him to his hands and knees.

In the sudden confusion of struggle and death, everything seemed to slow in Coyle's perception. The action around him appeared as some somber, mad dance. The noise even faded in his ears. Smoke and flame still spurted from the rifle barrels, horses and men screamed, but he heard nothing. Several yards away, Col. Forsyth tried to control his plunging horse in order to mount.

Coyle got to his feet and ran a few more steps. Suddenly, through the acrid smoke in front of him, he saw Big Foot, lying on his side. Blood stained his forehead.

"Father!" A young woman, wailing hysterically, threw herself down next to him. Even as Coyle stared, a bullet snapped her head sideways, and she fell limply on top of Big Foot.

Trying to get his bearings, Coyle turned stunned eyes toward the bulk of the fighting. Shooting and clubbing, the Indian men had breached the blue line of soldiers and made a rush out of the council circle, most of them dashing toward their own village beyond. In Coyle's slow perception of their movements, he caught sight of the brightly painted ghost shirt of Tom Merritt. Merritt had a pistol in his hand and was running with the knot of Indians who had broken through the line formed by K troop.

Molly! He made a dash toward the hill where he'd last seen her, his unfired Remington still gripped in his fist.

A dark figure lay on the ground several yards in front of him. Father Craft knelt at the side of a fallen private, making the sign of the cross on the soldier's forehead. From out of the murk a warrior leaped at the priest, driving a knife down into his back. A second later a soldier swung the stock of his carbine against the side of the Indian's head, smashing him down and out.

Coyle reeled toward the fallen priest, and yanked the bone-handled knife from his back. The black cassock was already shiny with blood. Father Craft pushed himself to a sitting position, gasping. Coyle expected to see him topple over dead. But the blue-eyed priest wiped a hand across his face and said: "I'll be all right. I have to get to the other wounded." To Coyle's amazement, he got to his feet and lurched away.

Overcoming some of his shock, Coyle dashed toward the hill. "Molly! Molly!" His voice was lost in the roar of battle as soon as it left his lips. He crouched beneath the thick pall of spent gunpowder and searched frantically, but she was nowhere on the hillside. He sprinted upslope toward the crest of the hill, wondering why he didn't hear the bellow of the Hotchkiss guns above him. Lungs laboring, he finally reached the top of the rise and fled past the batteries.

"I can't fire without hitting our own men!" one of the gunners yelled. "They're all mixed up down there!"

As he turned, Coyle was nearly trampled by

Col. Forsyth's black gelding as the officer yanked his mount to a stop and leaped down. The terrified animal bounded away, dragging his reins. "Get those guns ready!" he yelled at the artillerymen and Lt. Hawthorne. "A bunch of 'em broke the lines and are almost to their camp."

Coyle was barely aware of the gun crews wheeling the cannons around and depressing the barrels.

"Fire!"

The gunners yanked their lanyards, and the breechloaders boomed and bucked, belching clouds of smoke. Coyle heard the shells exploding and looked to see a canvas lodge dissolve in smoke and flame. The four guns kept up a continuous fire. Shells and shrapnel were whistling in all directions, the impersonal rain of death cutting down the fleeing Indians — women, children, men — and their ponies and dogs like wheat before a scythe. Two pursuing bluecoats stumbled and fell as well. Horses and mules were struck or grazed, stampeding in every direction. The Indian pony herd had broken loose. Panicked teams sped through, bouncing driverless wagons over rough ground and spilling their contents as they went. Even as Coyle looked, an exploding shell blew a wagon into splintered fragments, wheels flying into the air.

"Molly! Molly!" he shouted, a sinking feeling in his stomach.

"Thad! Here!" came the answering voice.

He saw that she had made her way to the top of the hill and flattened herself on the ground twenty yards behind the gun batteries, where stray bullets were not likely to find her.

"Oh, Molly, you're safe!" he cried, sliding down beside her.

"My God, Thad, what's happening? What started it?" She looked stunned, her wide eyes on him.

He shook his head. "I don't know. But there's no stopping it now."

"Don't fire! Those are squaws!" came a shout from the battery behind them. The guns fell suddenly silent. Coyle could hear the cursing of an artillery sergeant.

"Now! Here come the bucks! Let 'em have it!" an officer shouted.

The ear-slamming concussion of the four rifled cannons drowned all other noises. Coyle took Molly's hand, and they ran, crouching, toward the south side of the flat-topped hill. Several seconds later they saw a stream of Indians of all ages and both sexes break through, running toward a gully. The Indians gradually disappeared into the partial protection of this ravine, the bucks firing back at the soldiers as they ran. They were scrambling west along the bottom of the ravine, desperately seeking any shelter they could find.

The Indian scouts and the cavalry companies stationed beyond the ravine reined up and fell back as exploding shells began falling perilously close to them.

From where they lay prone on the cold earth, Coyle could see soldiers falling here and there, struck by bullets from the unseen Indian riflemen in the gulch. About two hundred yards south of their position, the gully made a sharp bend from west to south. Most of the rifle fire was coming from the pocket formed by that bend. Many fleeing Indians had stopped there in the relative protection of the sheer dirt bank and were fighting back. Their fire was deadly accurate. Lt. Hawthorne and Col. Forsyth noticed it, also, and began lobbing artillery rounds into this corner. Clouds of dust and smoke exploded into the air. There was no direct line of fire, but shell fragments must have been doing terrible damage because the keening of death chants rose from the gully between the sporadic crack of rifle fire. Two or three dozen soldiers, both on foot and horseback, were in hot pursuit along the edge of the ravine. Two officers were trying to call them back from exposure to the Indian fire.

Coyle saw two men struggling to roll one of the Hotchkiss guns off the gradual incline toward an opening to the gully. Bullets kicked up dust all around them, and holes appeared in the wooden wheel spokes, while the two soldiers scrambled to aim the gun and thrust a shell into the breech.

The battle raged for several more minutes — minutes that seemed like an hour.

"Let's get out of here!" Molly shouted in his ear. She jumped up. "Maybe we can get back to the post office."

"No! Not yet. We're safer here!" Coyle cried, shoving his pistol into its holster. He jumped to his feet and went after her.

An invisible fist struck him in the left side, knocking the wind out of him, and suddenly his right shoulder was plowing through the tangled grass.

"Thad! Thad!"

He could hear Molly, screaming his name, and wondered why she sounded so hysterical. He was lying on his side, gasping for breath. Then he felt a warm wetness inside his shirt, and the realization came to him that he'd been shot. His hat had rolled away on the ground, and sun blinded his eyes. He could see only the silhouette of the woman crouching above him.

"Where are you hit?" There were tears in her voice.

A few moments after the first shock, his mind became clear. He felt a dull pain in his left side, as if he'd been struck by a club. But he didn't feel any pain deep inside. His abdominal muscles were numb, almost paralyzed. He struggled to breathe, steeling himself against a stinging, burning sensation in several places nearer the surface.

He tried to speak, but couldn't seem to get the words out. He tried to rise, but Molly pushed him gently over onto his back. He was aware she was busy unbuttoning his vest and shirt. Her hands were shaking. "Oh, God! Where's the doctor?" he heard her saying, over and over.

The din of battle — the yelling of commands, the firing, the squealing of horses, the high-pitched death songs — had all faded into the background, as if this were taking place elsewhere, instead of all around them.

Coyle felt her cool fingers probing the bare flesh of his side. Finally she said: "You have eight or nine small holes in you. From this. . . ." She held up his watch by its chain. The thick, encased nickel-silver timepiece had taken a direct hit and was now only a twisted, jagged piece of metal. He reached up and took it from her. The bullet had penetrated nearly all the way through, driving the cogs and springs and metallic fragments into his side. These little projectiles were what he felt. The bullet itself, a distorted lump of lead, he touched with his thumb, and it fell out of a hole in the back of the case. "Thank God!" he breathed. He let the watch drop to the end of its chain. Then he rolled over and started to rise.

"Lie still. You may be bleeding internally," she said.

In spite of considerable pain, he squirmed around and pulled aside his bloody shirt to inspect the damage. Six or seven small, oozing holes marred the pale flesh. He lay back, wondering if any of those shards of metal or glass had penetrated the abdominal cavity or his kidneys. His head was clear, and the pain was tolerable. Fear and shock caused him to break into a cold sweat all over his body. He felt a chill from the dampness.

Coyle took a deep breath, while Molly slid his knife from his belt sheath and cut off the tail of his white shirt. She folded it to form a thin pad, pressing it against his skin, then fastened his cartridge belt over the shirt and vest to hold the makeshift compress in place. With unsteady fingers, he buttoned his corduroy jacket.

"That should help for now," she said. "But you need to lie still until the bleeding stops."

He was suddenly aware that all had become

quiet. At least, the noise of guns had ceased. It was a relative quiet, since he could still hear voices yelling in the distance, horses galloping, the shrill wailing of the death chants.

Holding his side with one hand, he rolled over and struggled to his feet.

"Where are you going?" She seemed alarmed.

"The fighting has stopped. I've got to see what happened."

"You're shot. You have to wait for the doctor."

He gasped as he straightened up, hand pressed to his side. "It was my watch that was shot and killed. I'm very much alive." He could feel beads of perspiration beginning to collect and run down his face. To put up a good front for her, he made no attempt to wipe his face. "Besides, the two surgeons will have their hands full. If you can help me to your buggy and hitch up, we can make it back to Pine Ridge on our own."

She bit her lip, and looked at him.

"Come on. Give me a shoulder to lean on."

As they started to move away, the first thing they saw made Coyle's queasy stomach want to vomit. Phillip Wells, his face a mass of blood and his nose still dangling, was jogging on foot along the lip of the ravine, yelling something over and over in Lakota.

"What's he saying?" Coyle asked.

"I can only catch some of it, but I think he's telling the Sioux to come out of hiding and they will not be shot."

Coyle and Molly paused to watch as singly, then in twos and threes, the Indians began to climb out of the gully, some bloody, others aiding the wounded to walk. About fifty troopers were sent in to help carry out the wounded. Forsyth came striding up to watch as the men and women gave up their guns and approached, hands raised. Some younger women had children by the hand or in their arms.

"Let's keep walking," Coyle said to Molly, leaning heavily on her. "If I'm walking, there is pain. If there is pain, I know I'm still alive."

She turned her head to look into his eyes, but said nothing. They walked west, away from the cannons toward the back of the flat hill where it gradually sloped downward. They came closer to the surrendering Indians until Coyle could see the details of their torn and dirty clothing, the red stains on sleeves and dresses.

About forty yards away, an Indian man, obviously wounded, pushed himself up on his arms. "By God, it's Tom Merritt!" Coyle gasped.

"Where?"

"That man up ahead there, on the ground. We have to help him."

Just then, a detail of cavalry came galloping over a rise toward them. One of the soldiers, seeing Tom Merritt attempting to get up, raised a revolver and shot him as they galloped past. Merritt flopped forward on his face.

"No!" The anguished cry was wrenched from Coyle's lips.

"For God's sake, stop shooting at them!" Forsyth roared, running up to the approaching horsemen.

"I'm sorry, sir," the cavalryman said, reining up. "We were out sweeping the area west of here. Didn't hear your order."

Coyle slowly, painfully, made his way toward the prostrate figure of Tom Merritt.

Molly eased him down to his hands and knees, then stepped back as Coyle crawled the last few feet to his old friend. "Tom . . . why did you come back here?" he whispered to the unhearing ears of the dead man. "We never got a chance to talk. You had made another life. Why? Why?" The sight of the bloody ghost shirt swam in his vision as tears filled his eyes. He took a deep breath, and felt the sharp pains of his own wounds. "You . . . of all people . . . the last one to die in this stupid fight!"

Chapter Nineteen

January 3, 1891
Battlefield at Wounded Knee

Molly Seeker drew her team of horses to a halt and let her gaze drift over the bleak, snow-covered prairie before her. Her gloved fingers and exposed face were numb after the eighteen-mile drive in the open buggy, but she hardly noticed. Had it been only five days since that violent struggle had taken place here? Already the details were hazy, as if it had occurred a long time ago. Or was it only the half-remembered terror of some nightmare?

She probably should have stayed at Pine Ridge and continued to help nurse the wounded, both Indian and white. But it had become too much for her. After two days of constant work and little sleep, preparing sandwiches and coffee, boiling water to wash bandages and clothing, keeping the fire going in her stove day and night for heat and cooking soup, she just had to get away. She made sure Thad was resting comfortably, then sought the cold air to clear her senses of the pitiful sights, sounds, and smells of the injured and dying.

In her mind's eye she could still see the interior of Holy Cross Episcopal church. The pews had been torn out and the floor strewn with straw. She and other whites at the agency had taken blankets and quilts from their beds to cover the straw before the wounded Indians were laid in two long rows on the floor. A Christmas tree had been removed, but wreaths and garland still decorated the walls where, ironically, the faithful had only a few days before celebrated the birth of the Prince of Peace. But it was the smell she remembered most vividly. In place of the usual scent of pine wreaths, a faint aroma of cedar, and the lingering fragrance of incense, she would now forever associate the little wooden church with the smell of putrefying wounds, excrement, carbolic acid, and damp straw, along with the moans and cries of pain. The church held thirty-six wounded Lakotas. The rest were housed in other buildings wherever there was room. But the most severely injured were on the floor of the little church. Dr. Hoff, bleary-eyed from constant work, had remarked to her that he estimated about two-thirds of them would die from shock or infection. Dr. Hoff had been forced to replace his uniform with civilian clothing before some of the Indian women would let him approach them. The two Army surgeons, along with Dr. Charles Eastman, the full-blood Santee Sioux, were making heroic efforts to save as many of the wounded as possible, and she admired them for their efforts. She was still taken with Dr. Eastman, a handsome, intelligent man with thick black hair and smooth, bronze skin.

She sat, hands tucked inside her coat, and breathing the frigid air as she let the horses rest for several minutes. It was good to get away from Pine Ridge. She had nowhere to go. But something had drawn her back to the battlefield at Wounded Knee Creek. A blizzard, followed by a blast of Arctic air, had blown in on the last day of December, and the temperature now hovered near ten degrees. The landscape before her was covered with four inches of crusty snow. Except for the litter of broken wagons, skeletal frames of burned-out lodges, and dark lumps of frozen corpses and dead horses, she would not have recognized this as the same place. Looking small in the distance, dark figures on horseback and afoot moved slowly about the vast snowscape.

Molly climbed down stiffly from the buggy, tied the team to a nearby bush, and walked back and forth for several minutes, stamping her feet and swinging her arms to restore circulation. Finally she began to feel the burning sensation of blood coursing back into her numbed fingers and toes. She went to the buggy and fumbled under the seat for a blanket-sided canteen, uncapped it, and swallowed some of the tepid coffee. Then she unwrapped a blue-checked napkin, took out half a sandwich, and began to munch on it — thick slices of homemade bread with butter and bacon between. The food seemed to warm her insides. Even though a weak sun struggled to show itself through a pale overcast, it failed to moderate the sharp north wind cutting her face.

She was thankful the weather had not been as severe the day she'd driven Thad back to the agency in her buggy. Wrapped in his buffalo coat, he'd sat hunched over on the seat beside her, silently enduring the jolting ride. She'd put him to bed in his own room in the agent's house and called in the storekeeper's wife to help bathe and nurse him. That evening, the flood of wounded Indians and soldiers in wagons and Army ambulances had arrived, and one of the surgeons had briefly examined Thad. He was painfully, but not mortally, damaged by the pieces of watch in his body, the surgeon had said. But it would take several operations and some careful probing to remove all the tiny scraps of metal. Even with a solid constitution, he was likely to be laid up for two or three weeks. What then? Molly pondered their future relationship. Thad was probably the best man she'd ever met — strong, kind, intelligent. He was a good fifteen years older — a fact she considered no great obstacle. But he was married. He had told her he'd been separated for a few years, yet had not indicated a divorce was anticipated.

She thrust the thought from her mind. Time for all that later. She rubbed the tip of her nose with a gloved hand. Untying the team, she climbed back onto the buggy seat, covering her lap and legs with a blanket. There was plenty of activity on the wide expanse ahead of her. She'd been told at Pine Ridge that the Army had hired local civilians to gather all the Indian dead and bury them in a mass grave. She wondered what kind of men would accept such a gruesome job, even for two dollars a body. The idea intrigued her. Would it be men who hated and feared the Lakotas and believed they'd gotten what they deserved? Or would it be compassionate men who felt they were performing a Christian work of mercy? Maybe they were just local ranchers who needed some cash to see them through the winter. There was no way of knowing what was in their minds as she drove her buggy slowly down among the workmen, all of them mustached, rough-looking. They glanced curiously at her as she went by, looking up from under hat brims, all of them wearing a nondescript assortment of jackets, neckerchiefs, vests, topcoats, suspenders over wool shirts, and cotton or rawhide work gloves.

She recognized the figure of Big Foot. He was inclined on his back, still wearing an overcoat and a scarf tied over his head, both arms partially upraised, as if he were trying to sit up and say something. In order to be in that posture, he must have fallen on his face, and then been turned over for a photograph, she thought. He was rigid as a board she realized, when two workmen grabbed his arms and wrenched his body loose from the crusted snow. They heaved his stiff corpse into a farm wagon, atop a pile of bodies frozen in grotesque shapes.

She was glad she'd already eaten her small lunch; her close-up view of the battleground had taken its toll on her stomach.

She kept the team moving at a slow walk, seeing more wagons and similar groups of men gathering the scattered bodies from where they had fallen and remained for three days. There appeared to be more than a hundred corpses. Where was Yellow Bird — the man whose provocative chanting and actions had helped set off the spark that led to all this? She'd heard a couple of soldiers at Pine Ridge talking about Yellow Bird's shooting from inside Big Foot's Sibley tent through a tiny hole. He had been finally noticed by one of the gunners who sent an exploding shell in that direction, shredding the tent, blowing up the coal oil for the stove, and incinerating Yellow Bird.

Two commercial photographers she knew from Rushville and Chadron were shooting pictures as fast as they could rush their bulky cameras and tripods from one grisly scene to another. One of them was also using a smaller, twin-lens camera. Images of the Wounded Knee dead would soon be showing up as three-dimensional stereopticon views in the parlors of genteel America.

What a horrible outcome to all this ghost dance business! And just when everyone thought it was going to end peacefully. Many good people, Lakotas and soldiers, women and children dead or wounded for no good cause. She had examined the posted list of Army casualties. Among those killed was First Sgt. Gustave Korn, caretaker of Comanche. Capt. George Wallace, a kind, congenial

man who'd struggled to bridge the gap between cultures, had had the top of his head
blown off in the first few minutes of the
fight. On the other hand, a man like Thomas
Carson had escaped without a scratch, and
had even gotten a scoop on all the big-city
papers. There was no way to make sense of it.
Maybe justice was reserved for the afterlife; it
certainly appeared that blind chance ruled the
earthly affairs of men.

Combing the battlefield ahead of the burial
parties were at least two dozen relic hunters.
With a profound sense of outrage, she
watched them snatching up everything —
moccasins, pipes, blankets, ghost shirts,
headdresses, feathers. Scavengers were op-
portunists who knew that the prices for such
artifacts would shoot skyward in the next days
and weeks. It seemed to her the final indig-
nity, but she had no power to stop it. Cavalry-
men, swathed in overcoats and fur hats, sat
their horses in small groups here and there,
turning a blind eye to the looters. She supposed the military was here to prevent any re-
prisal attacks from bands of roaming Indians
who had escaped. Not an unreasonable fear,
she thought, since such an attack had already
happened near the Catholic mission just four
miles north of Pine Ridge. At the first news of
the Wounded Knee clash, many Lakotas at

Pine Ridge had fled in panic. Kicking Bear's ghost dance hold-outs were camped nearby on their way to the agency, and they, too, started back for the Badlands. Both soldiers and civilians knew that several groups of these frustrated, fearful warriors, bent on revenge, had set fire to a day school and some out-buildings near the mission. While many of the whites, fearing an attack, barricaded them-selves in the Episcopal church rectory, Col. Forsyth had led part of the 7th cavalry to in-vestigate the smoke that could be seen from Pine Ridge. The troopers engaged the out-numbered Indians in a running battle. Appar-ently, through some blunder, Forsyth had gotten his men pinned down in a cañon. A troop of the black 9th cavalry had to make a forced march of more than forty miles to res-cue them.

General Nelson Miles had arrived from Rapid City four days ago to take personal charge of the situation. Thad said Miles was looking for a scapegoat to blame for the Wounded Knee disaster. Forsyth's tactical mistakes had provided that scapegoat.

She sighed, blowing out white vapor in the frosty air. It was a scheming, crazy, violent world. Maybe that was why she preferred to teach children who still retained a good por-tion of their innocence. It was her way of not having to deal with adult society.

She swung back onto the agency road, noted Mousseau's deserted store, and the locked post office. Then, on a whim, she angled her team to the left, off the road to the southwest, past the vacated cavalry camp, across the field where the Indian pony herd had been held. Then she continued up a long gradual slope that brought her to elevated ground. It was a hundred yards behind the hill where she and Thad had crouched and where he'd been shot.

Scattered over the field ahead were a half dozen bodies — dark lumps in the snow the burial party had not yet reached. Was one of them Tom Merritt? Would she even recognize Thad's old friend? She'd seen him only that once, when he was wounded, just before he'd been shot down before their eyes. If she could retrieve his body and bring it back to the agency for decent burial, Thad would be very grateful. A Christian funeral would be in order. Thad had told her this man had been a Presbyterian, then converted to the Episcopalian faith more than ten years ago.

She tried to orient herself and remember exactly where Merritt had fallen. She would examine all the bodies within a reasonable area. The cold would have preserved the features so they'd still be recognizable.

Some distance ahead of her, she saw a team and wagon roll to a stop, and two men get out, hauling tripods and cameras. As she got closer, she saw it was the outfit of George Trager, a photographer from Chadron, Nebraska. She didn't recognize the bigger man with him. Irritated, she realized they were just about at the spot where she planned to start her search. But she drove up near them, stopped, looped the reins around a metal brace on the seat, and stepped down. The two men briefly acknowledged her presence with a nod, but didn't interrupt their work. They were clearly in a hurry to catch the best light and to get the exposures they wanted before the burial party arrived. Walking in front of them, she bent to examine the face of a dead man. Dark blood crusted the back of his ghost shirt. With her gloved hand she brushed the snow from his features. He lay on his stomach with his face turned to one side, toward her. His eyes were closed, and he had a peaceful expression. The long hair was drawn back in a ponytail. Although somewhat discolored, the face was not disfigured, and, after she'd studied it for several seconds, she was certain it was Tom Merritt. Overcoming her instinctive revulsion, she straddled his body, put her hands under the arms, and lifted. Nothing happened. She braced her feet and heaved upward. With a ripping sound the rigid corpse tore loose, frozen grass and snow clinging to the underside.

"What the hell you doing, lady?" the bigger man barked, looking up from adjusting the legs of the tripod. "Get outta there. We want a picture of the way these Injuns fell!" he grated.

"I'm taking this man back to the agency for burial. He was a Christian."

"So what?" He waved a hand at the battlefield. "Most of these Injuns claimed to be . . . especially the ghosts dancers who were waitin' for the Messiah."

She didn't reply, but only began dragging the body toward her wagon. *Damn this heavy skirt,* she thought as the long wool folds impeded her movements.

"Whoa, there, missy. You ain't takin' that body nowhere until we make a view of it."

She stopped. "My name is Molly Seeker. I'm a teacher at Pine Ridge. And just who do you think you are?"

"Joe Ford. Me and George Trager, here, have teamed up to get some good, salable photographs for posterity."

She took an instant dislike to the overbearing manner of this big, rough-looking man. She paused and straightened up, stretching the muscles in her back. "I've known George

285

Trager for a long time. Does this man work for you, George?" she asked.

"Well . . . uh . . . there are some others we can get shots of, Joe, if she really wants this one. He doesn't look like a chief."

"He wasn't. His white name was Tom Merritt. He was a freighter in the Black Hills. His Lakota name was Swift Hawk."

"Oh, really? Then what was he doing here . . . and wearing a ghost shirt at that?" Trager asked.

Molly couldn't answer that, but her eyes fell on a pile of artifacts tossed behind the seat of their wagon — knives, eagle feathers, moccasins, and bloody ghost shirts. She could feel the warmth rising in her face. "I always thought you were a legitimate photographer, George," she said. "When did you take up scavenging relics from the dead?"

"Leave that body alone and step out of the way!" Ford commanded, moving toward her.

She took a step back and instinctively reached under her cape, drawing out a short-barreled Colt Lightning she'd brought along as protection against roving Indians.

Ford hesitated, looking at the .38 in her steady hand.

"Do you want this body badly enough to die for it?" Molly heard herself asking. She had no doubt she would pull the trigger if he tried physically to force her away.

"Take your body and get out of here," Trager intervened. "Come on, Joe. There's another one right over here we can get."

Trying to hide tears of rage and frustration, Molly holstered her Colt, seized the body of Merritt, and finished dragging him to her wagon. She stopped to take a quick breather and eyed the two men reloading their equipment into their wagon and talking angrily to each other. Molly couldn't make out their words.

She wondered if she could lift the body off the ground without help. But she found the slender Indian surprisingly light. Maybe it was because most of his blood had drained out. Or because he was not limp. She wrestled his stiff body onto the back floor of the buggy, then climbed up, and turned her team toward the agency road. She was still filled with rage at the insensitivity of the photographers. She would write a piece and send it to the newspapers to let the public know what vultures these people were. She felt she would surely get her article published if she gave an eyewitness account of the fight. And she was certainly articulate enough to write a good article.

She'd covered a mile or so with these thoughts whirling through her mind. Then anger began to ebb, and she started feeling the bite of the northwest wind she was driving into. It lashed tears from her eyes, and she tugged down the broad brim of her felt hat, letting the horses have their head to keep the road. Where would Tom Merritt's funeral be held? Holy Cross Episcopal church was being used as a hospital. Maybe Father Jutz would let them have the Catholic mission.

But then she began to wonder. Thad had not seen his friend for several years until a few days ago at Big Foot's side. And Merritt was wearing a ghost shirt. Had Merritt, formerly Swift Hawk, had a change of heart and religion and come back home to espouse the new quasi-Christian beliefs of the ghost dancers? It was entirely possible.

She looked back over her shoulder at the body. An empty holster was attached to the belt around the waist. It appeared he'd fought alongside his Lakota tribesmen when the fracas started. Even if he had not fought the soldiers, at least he hadn't run away, like many others. A thought gradually took shape in her mind, and she pulled the walking team to a halt. After many years away, perhaps he had come home to stay.

She snapped the reins and pulled the team around in a tight circle, back the way they'd come. If he'd come home to be with his people, and died helping them, wouldn't he want to be buried with them?

Twenty minutes later she drew up near the crest of the hill from where the Hotchkiss guns had rained down devastation on the Indian camp and ravine below. Several soldiers on foot stood guard with rifles, while six civilians threw shovelfuls of dirt up out of the long trench that was being excavated on the hilltop. She climbed down from her buggy. "I have another body for you," she said to one of the nearby soldiers who had approached to see what she wanted. "He's in the buggy."

"Charley, come get this body," the soldier called to one of the workmen who had just climbed out of the trench and was scraping mud from his boots. The man walked over and looked curiously at Molly. "Didn't know there was any women on this crew," he remarked, reaching in, grabbing Merritt by the legs, and yanking him out onto the ground.

"I'm not part of your crew. And treat that body with some respect!" she said, sharply. "He was a friend," she lied. "A good man." She was taking Thad's word on this.

"There are a lot of good men . . . women and children, too . . . going into this hole," one of the grave diggers called up from his position in the trench as he leaned on his shovel and wiped a shirt sleeve across his face.

289

"Put him on that stack over there," another man said, holding a pad of paper clipped to a board. "I'll have to get an accurate count before we start putting 'em under."

Molly took one last look at the rigid remains of Tom Merritt and noted that he was barefoot. She recalled Coyle removing Merritt's moccasins just after he died, as a tangible remembrance of his old partner.

She stopped and picked up a handful of snow and scrubbed it between her hands to clean the dirt and smudges of congealed blood from the leather gloves. Then, without a word, she got into her buggy and turned once again to face the bitter wind and the long trip home. But now, knowing she had done the right thing, her mind was at peace.

Chapter Twenty

January 9, 1891
Agent's House, Pine Ridge

Thad Coyle rolled over with a groan and swung his feet to the cold pine floor, then paused a few seconds, waiting for the sudden dizziness to pass.

The pain in his side had needled him awake sometime earlier in the black, pre-dawn hours. The hurting from yesterday's probing surgery was more of an aggravation than real pain, so he ignored the laudanum solution the doctor had left on his bedside table.

A new January day was creeping up over the Dakota plains. Although the sky was overcast, the daylight sliding through the windowpane owed much of its brightness to a reflection off the snow-covered land. Moving carefully to keep from pulling the stitches, Coyle reached for his pants on the bedpost and slid them on over his long johns. Then, with some difficulty, he managed to bend over far enough to pull on a pair of moccasins he'd been wearing in place of his heavy boots.

The sight of the tan deer hide, decorated with dyed green quills, brought thoughts of Tom Merritt who had last owned and worn this footgear. When, on impulse, he'd slipped them from his friend's feet as a keepsake, he had never thought he'd be wearing them himself.

He moved to the basin and poured in some water. The face looking back from the mirror above the washstand was whiskery, hollow-eyed and showed every one of its nearly fifty years. "Good God!" he muttered aloud. "I look like a burned out old reprobate!" He grinned at the thought, white teeth softening the grim visage. "Maybe I won't ignore the next panhandler I see on the street in Washington . . . he might be an old civil servant."

Molly had shaved him a week ago, but he was badly in need of another one. And a good, soaking bath would feel good as well. But he had to depend on someone else to help with that, since he wasn't yet capable of pumping and boiling the water by himself. But the bath would have to wait; the surgeon didn't want any dirty water getting into the small incisions he'd left open.

Out of habit, he reached for his pocket watch, then remembered that the shattered Elgin lying on the washstand was the reason he was still alive — and hurting. At least three more minor operations would be needed to remove the shards of metal from his side, he'd been told. He wondered why the doctor couldn't get all the pieces at one time. True enough, he'd dulled his sensitivity with whisky and oozed sweat from every pore when the doctor was cutting and probing. But he thought he probably could have withstood the pain a little longer, just to have the whole thing over with. The hangover from the unaccustomed hard liquor had been the worst of it. But he realized the doctor could work on him only during infrequent intervals between attending more severely injured patients.

The *bang* of a door, slamming in the front of the house, was followed by several loud voices and the thumping of men stamping snow from their boots.

"Damn," Coyle muttered, pushing the bedroom door shut. General Nelson Miles and his staff had just entered. Since his arrival about ten days before, the general had been using the agent's house as his headquarters. Royer had been evicted and was sleeping in his office. Miles reluctantly allowed Coyle to remain in his room because of his wounds.

He splashed water on his face, dried it on his sleeve, and ran a comb through his hair.

The *clink* of glassware and frying pans told him breakfast was being prepared for General

Miles and his senior staff. He could use some coffee, he thought, but wasn't yet hungry. His side was still sore, but he was definitely on the mend. He'd slept pretty well, and felt stronger than he had in days. Dirty, jagged pieces of metal — Dr. Hoff had said there was a good chance infection would develop. But it hadn't. Lucky, the doctor said, even though he was very careful to disinfect everything and left the wounds open to drain and heal from the inside out — except for the larger incision he'd had to stitch five days earlier.

Coyle unbuttoned and peeled down the top of his red cotton long johns, then set about changing the dressings. There was no odor or pus. "Laudable pus" physicians used to call it, mistakenly thinking its formation was a sign of the body healing itself. Coyle smiled at how far science had come as he dosed the wounds with carbolic and re-bandaged his side with gauze and clean cotton bandages Molly had left him, tying the cotton strips around his waist.

When he finished, he sat in a wooden armchair and rested for several minutes, staring out at the snowy landscape, the water tower, and the top of the boarding school where Molly was probably working this morning with others to get the school ready to reopen.

His stomach growled, and he started to get

up, put on his shirt and coat, and go down the street to breakfast. But he delayed, continuing to gaze out the window at the tranquil winter landscape and the few small, leafless trees near the house. Now that the Sioux had been conquered, he felt restless. His life seemed to lack direction. He needed some sort of immediate goal to work toward. For the most part, he'd always been a practical man of action, with little time given to introspection. The times he'd let himself sink below the surface to examine his deeper emotions were times of pain and regret, usually associated with his marriage. He was fearful of what he'd find in the shadows of his own soul. He pictured the darker side of human nature as something to be kept under control lest it burst forth like a volcano, manifesting itself in such things as wars and insane asylums. He sighed. It seemed the longer he lived, the less he really knew himself. He'd gotten along by learning to trust his instincts, rather than his analyses. Better to deal with things as they appeared rather than looking for hidden motives.

The last few days, during his enforced idleness, he'd begun to feel uneasy. At first he put it down to the blues brought on by being shot. But now he'd begun to realize it was a natural letdown following the end of the Indian resistance. The ghost dance craze had festered for months, grown sore and redder and angrier until it had finally burst open at Wounded Knee. There were still daily alarms and random shots fired at the agency, and hold-out Lakotas who refused to surrender, but it was essentially over. And the wounds of the bodies, of the land, and of the spirit were already beginning to heal. The Sioux had been finally and thoroughly crushed at last. There would be no more active resistance — at least, not in his lifetime.

Restlessly, he got up and retrieved his shirt from a wooden peg on the back of the door. He stared, unseeing, at the wall while his mind groped for answers.

What would he do with his life now? He had come very close to death. Would he just let his wounds heal, and then go back to the routine of his job in the Indian Bureau? The tension and excitement that had been sustaining him for the better part of a year was gone. He realized now, more than he had for months, that his life was essentially a lonely one. Some men had hobbies such as a passion for sporting events like boxing or horse racing, or some other form of gambling that stimulated their senses and filled the hours away from work. He had no such recreation save an interest in collecting and studying artifacts from various Indian tribes he'd encountered. Lacking a family, maybe it was time to pull himself together and develop some outside interests, to refocus on something else besides his job.

What about Molly and Emma? Emma was content to live apart from him and correspond by letter like a friend. Molly had her job here — a definite purpose in life in helping to civilize the next generation of Lakotas. What did he think of each of them? The two women were entirely different in looks, personality, and temperament. Molly had shown the greater interest in him, yet had never mentioned marriage or leaving the reservation. Without being pushy about it, she presented herself as a very independent female. But, perhaps, she was only waiting for a proposal. How would Emma react to mention of a divorce? Would she fight it and try to block it and generally make his life hell as she had done in the past? He knew he should be more sensitive to women's needs and views, but, like most men he'd known, he just didn't have the capacity of seeing things from a woman's perspective. Maybe it was simply nature's way.

His thoughts turned from this conundrum to Tom Merritt. Molly had described her trip to the battlefield, and he completely agreed with her decision to leave Merritt's body for burial with his Lakota people. "I just regret we didn't get to talk before he was killed," he'd told her. Now he would never know for sure why Merritt had chosen to return and ally himself with his kin in Big Foot's band of Miniconjous.

He went over details of the fight in his memory. The sight of Phillip Wells with his nose sliced off came to mind. Instead of being disfigured for life, or bleeding to death, the tough interpreter had continued to function until the end of the battle, finally calling for the surrender of the Indians in the ravine. Sometime later, one of the surgeons had sewn the nose back on, and it was apparently doing fine.

While he put on his shirt and buttoned it, he reflected on the strong opinions he'd heard from several of the Lakotas during the past ten days. They had been blaming the provocative actions of Yellow Bird for starting the fight. Coyle saw these accusations as human nature trying to simplify a very complex sequence of events, involving many people, that had led up to the battle. He doubted seriously if any one person could have caused or prevented what happened.

He reached over to the washstand for an envelope and slipped a folded letter from it.

Holding it to the light from the window, he read the message again with mixed feelings. It had been delivered yesterday by a young Indian boy. The letter was about the last thing Coyle ever expected to receive, and he wasn't completely sure how to take it. Things were never black and white, and human beings never ceased to surprise him. It was a note from Thomas Carson. Written in a hasty scrawl, it read:

I am leaving by stage today for Rushville to catch the train to Omaha. I won't pretend to like you, but, given enough time, things come around full circle. I want to thank you for saving me from the ghost dancers. In return for this, I will not say or write anything about your court-martial and dishonorable discharge. I don't know how you managed to hide it all this time, but if the facts about your past ever reach your bosses, you can believe I had nothing to do with it.

Three of us reporters witnessed the battle and came away unscathed. Within the hour, we wrote our first-person accounts in Mousseau's store near the battlefield. By luck of the draw, my dispatch was first to be put on the wire from Rushville. As a result, I will receive national recognition and a substantial raise and promotion.

I can't forget everything that's happened between us, but I wish you no harm. I hear that your wounds are superficial and you will recover. So be it. With any luck, we'll never meet again.

Yours,
Thomas Carson

For Carson, this was a very conciliatory message. It was obviously written in the flush of victory when he could afford to be generous. Yet, he hadn't had to write it at all. As he folded the single sheet and put it back into the envelope, Coyle had to admit to a grudging admiration for the man. Nobody was all good or all bad, but, according to their various traits, individuals either got along, or they didn't. Coyle smiled to himself — maybe Carson was following the scriptural advice to heap coals of fire on the head of your enemy by being kind to him.

What Carson said about events coming full circle was probably right. Coyle's clash with Carson and the military was the reason for his being here. And it had started fifteen years ago in Nebraska, less than two hundred miles from where he now sat. When one was able to back up and view them from a distance, the cycles in men's lives seemed to mirror other cycles in nature.

Enough of this. He got up, donned the buffalo coat, his broad-brimmed hat, and went out the front door by way of the hall, avoiding the general and his staff in the dining room.

The bite of the wind on his naked face felt good as he walked slowly along the snow-packed street, favoring his side. At the Hotel de Finlay he enjoyed pancakes and bacon washed down with three cups of hot coffee.

It was amazing what a little hot food could do for a man's outlook on life, he thought, as he headed for a barbershop that had opened since the soldiers came, obviously just to take advantage of the temporary boom in trade. It was in a ramshackle wooden building that had been vacant.

"I just opened up. You're the first customer of the day," the lean barber said, stepping out of his own barber chair — actually a rocker that could be tilted back at any angle by propping a log under the front curve of the rockers.

"A shave and trim," Coyle said, shedding his buffalo coat. He was immediately aware of a definite chill in the air. There was a good reason this tiny building had been vacant — the warped boards let in outside air faster than the small oil stove could warm it.

Coyle sat down, and the barber swung a huge, striped drape over him, tucking it in around the collar.

"Joe Ford owns this place, doesn't he?" Coyle asked.

"Sure does. But he only comes in when the soldiers get paid. We're real busy then," the barber said, snipping his scissors rapidly in the air, as if to warm them up.

"He's a photographer, too?"

"That's his main line of work. But he does lots of things," the barber said.

And one of them is scavenging relics from dead bodies, Coyle thought, sure now that this was the same Joe Ford that Molly had clashed with.

"What'd you think of all that fighting over east of here?" The barber moved up behind him, combing and snipping. Coyle could smell a faint aroma of pomade hair tonic on the man.

"Pretty bad," Coyle said.

"I'm glad General Miles got here and took charge of things. He's got the soldiers dug in just north of the agency. Put up cannon there, too. Those red bastards are still running loose, shooting at agency buildings and attacking ranchers and soldiers just a few miles from here. But I feel a whole lot safer now, with the boys in blue entrenched around Pine Ridge."

Coyle muttered his assent, his mind elsewhere.

The barber continued his monologue as he finished cutting Coyle's thick hair. Then he dipped a towel into a pan of water, steaming on the oil stove. He gingerly wrung the towel out, wrapped it around Coyle's face, then began stropping his straight razor on a leather strap.

A quarter of an hour later, Coyle stepped out of the chair, and regarded himself in the mirror the barber held up. The lean face was once again smooth, and his dark hair was trimmed neatly around his ears and combed back in a semi-pompadour.

He paid the barber and tipped him for a job well done. Shrugging into the buffalo coat, he went outside and walked back up the street. A few of the Indians who had stayed at the agency were abroad on the street, along with several white civilians and soldiers. In spite of any upheavals, routine business, like nature, seemed to take over, once the excitement was past.

Approaching the agent's quarters, he heard the sound of martial music. The 1st infantry regimental band — all eighteen or twenty of them — were standing in a circle in the trampled snow, playing a military march. He stopped to watch and listen. By order of

General Miles, the band played for a half hour every day in front of the general's headquarters. Miles thought that music, along with the bugle calls, lent a sense of orderly military routine to Pine Ridge.

When they'd finished and marched away, Coyle went inside to a room that was part office, part library, and built a fire in the small fireplace, using wood from the nearly empty wood box. He sat down at the desk, rubbed his hands briskly together, and pulled the inkstand toward him, along with a wooden pen containing a new steel nib. The desk drawers furnished a stack of clean white sheets of paper.

This was part of his job that he detested and had put it off until the very last. He would have to furnish a full report of his activities and the happenings of his extended assignment to Pine Ridge. Government reports — the bane of his existence. But, as long as he was employed by the Indian Bureau, he had to furnish them to his superiors. It was almost as if his trips and activities did not exist until they were committed to paper — to be glanced at and filed away as justification that the taxpayers were getting their money's worth.

Once he got started, the writing would not be difficult; he'd had much practice at this and knew what was expected. He'd have to check some particulars with Royer and General Brooke, but he'd just stick pretty close to the facts, and keep all emotion and opinion out of it. He was expected, however, to furnish his official assessment of the situation — a summing up, as it were, at the end of his report. After all, he was a Special Indian Agent with considerable experience, and his opinion did carry some weight. But he didn't fool himself. No opinion, however expert, ever overrode political decisions. Expediency was the rule of this game. And that was exactly why the government's relations with all its Indian tribes had been so abysmal. This thought, of course, would never make it into his report.

He flipped up the lid of the brass inkstand and dipped the pen. Pausing thoughtfully, he stared at the blank paper. Coyle wondered, as he often did, how the fact of his court-martial had escaped the attention of his bosses. In the nine years he'd been with the Department of the Interior, he'd run into only a handful of men he'd known or served with in the Army, and these had been unaware of how his military career had ended. Yet, most of his higher bosses, if not honorable men, had at least been shrewd. They should have known about him, about how he'd lied on his application. It was likely someone had checked his background. Over the years he'd often suspected they *knew* he had a dishonorable discharge, and just didn't care. As long as they thought of him as capable and experienced, they would ignore the rutted road of his past. Most of his bosses probably had skeletons in their own closets as well.

Three hours later, he had covered several sheets with a firm, legible script, and had struck out only a few lines. Still, easy enough for a typist to read. He put down the pen and flexed his fingers. The room had grown chill again, and he got up to add a log to the fire.

He was crouched, poking up the blaze, when he heard the door open behind him. He rose and turned, then froze with shock. There stood Molly and Emma. He looked from one to the other, not knowing what to say. "By God!" he finally managed to gasp.

"She came to the office looking for you," Molly said, closing the door. "I'd finished at school for the morning and happened to be there, helping Royer."

"Well . . . ," Coyle said, coming toward them. "What are you doing here?" he asked Emma, realizing how bumbling and foolish he must appear. He stepped forward and gave her an awkward hug, glad he'd just been shaved and smelled of bay rum.

"I read in the paper about the battle and that you'd been shot," she replied hesitantly. "I had to come and see about you."

Coyle glanced at Molly, but could read nothing in her face.

"It's nothing. I'm OK. I was shot in the watch."

"The what?"

"The bullet hit my watch, and I've got a few pieces of metal in me."

"Oh."

"I don't mean to make light of it. It hurts like hell. And if it hadn't been for Molly, here, I might have bled to death, or the wounds might have festered, or . . . by the way, have you two met?"

"We introduced ourselves," Molly said.

"Here, sit down. Take off your coat," Coyle said, trying to get his balance. Neither woman had smiled since they entered the room.

"Well, how've you been?" Coyle asked Emma when they were all seated. He leaned back in the wooden armchair in front of the desk. This is what came of a man getting too comfortable. Enduring the pain of surgery would be preferable to facing this situation, he thought.

"Nothing's changed since I wrote you last month," Emma said.

Coyle didn't look at Molly. Would she think him a hypocrite for not mentioning that he and Emma had been corresponding?

"How are the kids?" Coyle asked, unable to think of anything else to say.

"Bradley likes his job as an apprentice steamfitter. And Jill is studying to be a teacher."

Coyle knew this, but was stalling as he studied her. There was some slight graying in her brown hair, and a few fine lines in her face, but she was still an attractive woman. She was wearing a wool travel outfit with a close-fitting jacket and a full skirt with high, laced shoes. The only jewelry was a cameo brooch at the throat of her ruffled shirtwaist and the plain golden wedding band. He dropped his eyes. So she still considered herself married. He was silent for several seconds.

"Royer's expecting me back," Molly said, rising and slipping her arms into her coat. "You two probably have a lot to talk about. I'll see you later."

When the door closed behind her, Coyle and Emma sat in an embarrassing silence for several long seconds.

He had somewhat recovered from the first shock, and determined that she should state her case first. He refrained from filling the empty air between them with even emptier words.

"I've missed you," she finally said in a low voice.

Sudden resentment at having missed his children's growing up and the imagined comforts of a wife and home boiled up within him. He nearly bit his tongue to keep from making a sharp retort.

But his feelings must have shown on his face as she said: "I know you must hate me. I don't blame you." She paused.

He kept silent, tapping his fingers on the pine desktop, and not looking at her. He didn't trust himself to speak, surprised at the sudden bitterness her presence had engendered. He took a deep breath. "Emma, what do you want of me this time?"

"I . . . uh. . . ." She cleared her throat. "When I read that you'd been shot, I realized how much I still loved you," she said in a low, strained voice. "I couldn't put that in a letter. I had to come in person."

Easy enough to say, Coyle thought. *Where were you when I really needed you, really loved you a few years ago?* But he said nothing, seeing her brown eyes filling with tears.

"Your wound made me see what a fool I've been. All the way here by train and then on the stage from Rushville, I was in agony, thinking I might find you unconscious or dead, and it would be too late for me to tell you this."

She was either a very good actress, or it was really hurting her to admit it. He decided the latter, since she'd always been brutally frank with him. Deviousness was not her style. But he wasn't going to make this any easier for her. He remained impassive.

"If you still have any feelings for me, I thought . . . maybe . . . we could try again."

God, he thought, he couldn't put himself through this again. If she was emotionally unstable, what was to prevent her from leaving once more? But the stresses on their lives had lessened. She had reared the children almost alone, and they had apparently turned out all right. He was financially stable now. Did he still love her? Deep down he did. Could he make a snap decision to live with her again? He would have to think that over.

She read his hesitancy as reluctance and went on: "There's probably something going on between you and that . . . that Molly."

"What makes you think so?"

"I saw the way she looked at you. She's younger, and very attractive, in an outdoor kind of way."

"Molly's a good friend," he said a little too abruptly. "She's helped me a lot in the months I've been here." Suddenly changing the painful subject, he asked: "Do you have a place to spend the night?"

She shook her head.

"I don't think there's a spare room anywhere in Pine Ridge. You can take my bedroom. I'll sleep in here on the sofa. Where's your luggage?"

"I just brought one small grip. It's in the hall."

"Hungry?"

"Uhn-huh." She nodded.

"We'll stash your bag and go down the street to get some lunch."

As they went out the door, Coyle determined to put off the big questions between them until they could talk and get reacquainted after a five-year absence.

Chapter Twenty-One

"Time to get you some fresh air."

Slouched, half asleep on the sofa, Coyle looked up at the voice. Molly was standing in the doorway of the small library. She wore a gray cape and held her big felt hat in her hands.

"What?"

"You and I are going on a picnic."

"Molly, it's the middle of January."

"Sun's up, snow's gone, and it's getting warmer," she replied briskly in a tone that brooked no argument. "Your wounds haven't bled for a week. Let's go. My buggy's outside, and I've got a lunch basket packed."

Besides putting the finishing touches on his report, all he'd done for several days was eat and sleep — and wonder what to do about Emma. She had left two days after she arrived, taking the stagecoach back to the train at Rushville. Nothing had been decided between them. He was still stirred by old feelings for her, but hard experience had made him wary. He stalled, telling her he would come to Cairo on the way back to Washington, and they'd discuss it further.

He got up and stretched, feeling the tightness in his side. Even though weak and tired, he was healing nicely. Dr. Hoff had finished with him, but indicated he'd probably not gotten all the fragments out. One or more pieces might work their way to the surface in the next few months.

"Where we going?"

"Wounded Knee Creek."

He paused with one arm in the sleeve of the buffalo coat. "I'm not sure I'm ready for that."

"We'll see. Everything's pretty peaceful, but bring your Remington, just in case."

The fresh air sharpened their appetites, and they stopped to eat before reaching the battlefield. It was a level spot, close by several bare trees that bordered the ice-fringed creek, near enough to hear water gurgling over gravel in the shallows.

Cold fried chicken and potato salad were washed down with canteen water and a bottle of white wine from the trader's store. Coyle relished the food and gave only passing consideration to the thought that Molly had gotten him out here to talk about a subject he hadn't mentioned for a week — Emma. He would let her bring it up, if she intended to.

But she chatted only about routine things and the state of the Lakotas. "When I'm standing in front of those schoolchildren, I feel almost ashamed to be white, after what happened," she remarked, growing serious, as she started to put the remnants of food back into the basket.

"There were at least twenty-five soldiers killed, too," Coyle reminded her, sipping his wine from a metal cup. "And quite a few wounded. The Sioux even fired first. I was there."

"I know. I was there, too. But . . . it's such a tragedy. Especially with all those innocent children and women killed." She shook her head. "I'll never be able to get some of those sights out of my mind. One little boy about five years old was in the church. He'd had his throat shot to pieces. When they tried to give him food or water, it came right out the side of his neck."

"I'm sure my dreams will be haunted for months to come, too," Coyle agreed, handing her his empty cup. "Those ghost shirts didn't turn aside bullets, after all," he mused thoughtfully. "I wonder if most of them really believed they would?"

"Faith is a powerful force," she said. "If

they thought the white race would vanish from the earth and the buffalo would reappear, I guess it wouldn't be too hard to believe ghost shirts would protect them."

They rolled up their blanket and stashed it in the buggy, then resumed their drive.

The battlefield was deserted when they arrived an hour later. Nearly three weeks after the fight, the carcasses of dead horses still littered the field, but warmer weather and scavengers had already gone a long way toward reducing the remains to skeletons and hide. Some bare teepee poles stood to mark the site of the Indian camp. Molly halted the team, and Coyle climbed down. A ragged piece of canvas clinging to a tent pole was fluttering softly in the breeze, emphasizing the loneliness of the place. It seemed incongruous to Coyle that they should be out enjoying a ride and picnic as if nothing had happened here. But the gentle breeze spoke of recent ghosts in the silence. Neither of them talked for several minutes.

"Did you watch the council the other day?" Coyle finally asked, turning toward her.

"No. I was busy at school. And I wouldn't have wanted to see their humiliation anyway."

"Well, I was there. General Miles finally got most of the chiefs to come in for a long talk. He announced to the reporters next day that the war was officially over. He's scheduled a grand review of the troops for two days from now, with the band playing and colors flying."

"General Miles seems big on ceremony."

"It's not only that. The photographers and reporters will record it all. He wants to be sure he gets credit for the complete surrender of all the hold-outs, which he'll probably have within a few days. I understand he has Presidential ambitions. He needs all the good publicity he can get."

Molly got out of the buggy and walked around to stand beside him and look out over the field. "Are you going back to her?" she asked abruptly.

It was the question Coyle had been expecting all day.

"I've given it a lot of thought," he replied. "And I plan to give it one more try . . . if she'll come to live with me in Washington. I might apply for a transfer to finish out my career somewhere in the West." So there it was. He didn't believe in duplicity or vague answers.

She nodded, hardly changing expression, as if she'd expected it all along.

Coyle resisted the urge to soften the blow by telling her how much he thought of her. He didn't want to sound hypocritical, but he would have given anything to spare her feelings somehow at that moment.

"It's been a wonderful experience knowing you," she said simply.

When she kissed him lightly on the lips, Coyle found himself almost regretting his decision. They hugged silently for a few moments.

She backed away. "Ready to go?" she asked.

"Ready."

The sun showed a glint of wetness in her eyes just before he handed her up into the driver's seat.

The black buggy rolled west past the deserted log buildings along the agency road. Gradually the *clopping* of the horses' hoofs faded as team and buggy grew smaller in the distance.

A lone coyote trotted out of the trees along the creek. Moving quickly, he crossed the silent battleground, sniffing the remains of campfires whose charred wood still retained the faint hint of bacon grease. Head erect and alert, he trotted across the ravine and up the low hill, searching in the tangled, dead grass for scent of a possible meal.

Like a feathered projectile, the golden eagle hurtled out of the pale blue sky, hitting and killing a rabbit with one fatal thrust. The coyote froze, riveted by the brief flurry of feathers and fur in the grass forty yards ahead of him. With silky thrusts of powerful wings, the big raptor lifted himself back into the air, limp prey gripped in his talons.

The coyote watched for a moment as the eagle wheeled upwind to gain altitude. Then he turned and padded softly away down the slope toward the cover of trees along the stream.

All that remained was the eternal prairie wind, caressing the trampled grass and fluttering the tattered remnant of canvas clinging to a teepee pole. On the flat hilltop, wind whispered over a long, fresh scar in the earth — a filled trench that hid the remains of a Lakota dream.

Epilogue

Francis Craft, S.J., who was stabbed in the back during the battle, continued to minister to the wounded until he collapsed. He was laid up for a short time from the severe lung wound, but made a full recovery.

On January 26th, after the final surrender of the Sioux, General Nelson Miles issued orders for the reassignment of his regiments. As a precaution against further violence, he held the 1st infantry at Pine Ridge for another month before ordering them back to the West Coast.

Two officers investigating the Wounded Knee incident placed part of the blame on Col. James Forsyth. General Miles endorsed their findings and added some harsher comments of his own, accusing Forsyth of incompetence and neglect and of disregarding orders. The report was forwarded to the adjutant general in Washington on January 31st. Miles's superiors, however, ignored his recommendations for punishment of Col. Forsyth.

Daniel Royer was replaced as Indian agent

at Pine Ridge in early 1891.

A total of one hundred and forty-six Indians of all ages and both sexes were buried in the mass grave. An exact figure of casualties may never be known since evidence indicated the Lakotas carried away several of their dead and wounded.

As expected, the value of Wounded Knee relics shot skyward. Numerous ghost shirts, claimed by the sellers to have been worn by Big Foot, were sold for inflated prices. By an odd chain of events, one ghost shirt from the battle later wound up in a museum in Scotland. More than a hundred years later it was recognized by an American tourist, and negotiations were begun for its return. In a solemn ceremony, Scottish museum officials presented this ghost shirt to Lakota leaders at Wounded Knee in August, 1999.

Twenty-seven soldiers were awarded the Congressional Medal of Honor for their actions during the entire Wounded Knee campaign. One of these, a Corporal Paul Weinert, took the place of a fallen artilleryman and fired a Hotchkiss gun. During the fighting, he rolled the gun down toward the ravine where the Indians were retreating. As he described it later: "They kept yelling at me to come back, and I kept yelling for a cool gun . . . there were three more on the hill not in use. Bullets were coming like hail from the Indians' Winchesters. The wheels of my gun were bored full of holes, and our clothing was marked in several places. Once a cartridge was knocked out of my hand, just as I was about to put it in the gun, and it's a wonder the cartridge didn't explode. I kept going in farther, and pretty soon everything was quiet at the other end of the line."

Just after the fighting stopped, Phillip Wells returned to the council area where it had all started. In the shirt pocket of one of several dead warriors he found a religious tract perforated by the bullet that killed him. The title of the pamphlet was "The Kingdom of God Has Come Nigh Unto Thee."

Molly Seeker followed through on her vow to write a newspaper story. In it, she laid most of the blame on the military for the tragedy at Wounded Knee. Molly and Dr. Charles Eastman were later married and moved away from the reservation; he practiced medicine in other parts of the country. In addition to rearing their children, Molly continued to write for publication and was active in charitable causes.

The 7th cavalry horse, Comanche, died the following year, some say of grief at the loss of his long-time caretaker and friend, Sgt. Gustave Korn, who was killed at Wounded

Knee. On the other hand, Comanche *was* more than twenty years old. This hardy old horse was saved for posterity by being stuffed and is still on display in a Kansas museum.

A stone monument was built at Fort Riley, Kansas bearing the inscription: *To the soldiers who were killed in battle with Sioux Indians at Wounded Knee and Drexel Mission, South Dakota, December 29 and 30, 1890. Erected as a tribute of affection by their comrades of the Medical Department and Seventh cavalry, U.S. Army, A.D. 1893.*

In 1903, Joseph Horn Cloud, with help from friends and relatives, erected a monument at the side of the mass grave at Wounded Knee. The inscription includes the following: *Big Foot was a great chief of the Sioux Indians. He often said I will stand in peace till my last day comes. He did many good and brave deeds for the white man and the red man. Many innocent women and children who knew no wrong died here.*

Emma and Thaddeus Coyle managed to live more or less happily together until his death of heart failure in 1908 while he was still employed by the U.S. Department of the Interior.

About the Author

Tim Champlin, born John Michael Champlin in Fargo, North Dakota, was graduated from Middle Tennessee State University and earned a Master's degree from Peabody College in Nashville, Tennessee. Beginning his career as an author of the Western story with SUMMER OF THE SIOUX in 1982, the American West represents for him "a huge, ever-changing block of space and time in which an individual had more freedom than the average person has today. For those brave, and sometimes desperate souls who ventured West looking for a better life, it must have been an exciting time to be alive." Champlin has achieved a notable stature in being able to capture that time in complex, often exciting, and historically accurate fictional narratives. He is the author of two series of Westerns novels, one concerned with Matt Tierney who comes of age in SUMMER OF THE SIOUX and who begins his professional career as a reporter for the Chicago *Times-Herald* covering an expeditionary force venturing into the Big Horn country and the Yellowstone, and one with Jay McGraw, a callow youth who is plunged into outlawry at the beginning of COLT LIGHTNING. There are six books in the Matt Tierney series and with DEADLY SEASON a fifth featuring Jay McGraw. In THE LAST CAMPAIGN, Champlin provides a compelling narrative of Geronimo's last days as a renegade leader. SWIFT THUNDER is an exciting and compelling story of the Pony Express. WAYFARING STRANGERS is an extraordinary story of the California Gold Rush. In all of Champlin's stories there are always unconventional plot ingredients, striking historical details, vivid characterizations of the multitude of ethnic and cultural diversity found on the frontier, and narratives rich and original and surprising. His exuberant tapestries include lumber schooners sailing the West Coast, early-day wet-plate photography, daredevils who thrill crowds with gas balloons and the first parachutes, tong wars in San Francisco's Chinatown, Basque sheepherders, and the *Penitentes* of the Southwest, and are always highly entertaining. BY FLARE OF NORTHERN LIGHTS is his next Five Star Western.

The employees of Thorndike Press hope you have enjoyed this Large Print book. All our Large Print titles are designed for easy reading, and all our books are made to last. Other Thorndike Press Large Print books are available at your library, through selected bookstores, or directly from the publishers.

For more information about titles, please call:

(800) 223-1244

To share your comments, please write:

Publisher
Thorndike Press
295 Kennedy Memorial Drive
Waterville, ME 04901